No Time to Win

GREATER LIFE ROMANCE

ROBIN MERRILL

New Creation Publishing

Prologue

"Jada is a ball hog."

"Yes, Dad." Kyra already knew that Jada was a ball hog. Everyone did.

"So then stop giving her the ball."

Kyra swallowed hard and looked out her window. It was dark out, so she couldn't see anything but blurry blackness. "I have to give her the ball. It's the play that Coach taught us."

"Your coach is an imbecile. Good coaches don't coach sixth grade girls' basketball teams. And if you'd score once in a while, then the coach will make plays that put the ball in your hands. So pass to Jada less and shoot more."

Kyra couldn't do this. She didn't want to go against her coach, and she wasn't a very good shot.

Her father could read her mind. "You'd be a better shot if you'd shoot more. Practice makes perfect."

"Yes, Dad."

"Don't *yes, Dad* me. You want to be good, don't you? Otherwise, we're just wasting our time. And I can't afford to be wasting my time, or my gas money, following you all over the state if you're just going to run up and down the floor doing nothing."

"Yes, Dad." Oops, she'd done it again. "Sorry, Dad."

"Don't be sorry. I don't want your apologies. The Bible says it's better to obey than to sacrifice. Do you know what that means?"

Not really. "Yes."

"Good. Kyra, I only want what's best for you. And you know what's best for you? Your best. There's no point in participating if you're not going to do your best."

She bit her lip. She thought she had been doing her best.

"And another thing. I know you were happy that you made that foul shot, but it really doesn't count if you bank it in. And if you're not getting called for any fouls, then you're not working hard enough on defense. And ..."

Kyra watched the darkness whiz by her window and waited to get home.

Chapter 1

Coach Kyra Carter looked at the score clock at the end of the gym and tried not to show her frustration. She'd been working on her coaching-poker-face for eight years, but she couldn't do it yet.

She tried to get her shooting guard's attention, but all her girls were pretending they couldn't hear her. They knew they were stinking up the court. They knew she was furious. And they weren't going to let her tell them how to fix it.

"Daphne!" Kyra screamed hard enough to hurt. "Look at me!"

Daphne finally looked at her.

"You have to screen away!" Kyra hollered and pointed.

She knew how bad it sounded when she raised her voice like that. And it wasn't fair. When a male coach raised his voice, he sounded intimidating. Powerful. Commanding. No one ever accused him of being unprofessional. Or unhinged.

But when she hollered, she sounded like an emotional banshee.

Daphne nodded and trotted away.

Kyra tried to cool down. She glanced at the clock again. It was a nervous tic. And the clock said exactly what she'd known it would say.

Down by six.

To Reid State College.

This was ridiculous. Fort George had no business trailing Reid State. In anything. Ever.

They had no business trailing anyone, but certainly not Reid State. They should be crushing this team.

Yet here they were making turnovers and acting like they'd never run an offense before.

"Daphne is a mess," her assistant coach said quietly. "Do you want to put Ella in?"

"No," Kyra snapped. Ella on her best day couldn't compete with Daphne.

Coach Tamara Weiger leaned back in her chair, unoffended. She was used to Kyra's shortness.

With the back of her hand, Kyra dabbed the rebellious beads of sweat forming on her forehead. She didn't want to mess up her foundation, but she didn't want rivulets of sweat running down her forehead either.

Gross.

Another thing that wasn't fair. She was wearing a pantsuit while her girls got to wear shorts, even though she was working harder than they were. Right now anyway.

And why did her college pump so much heat into this gym when her winning record had fans packed in like hot sardines?

Finally, Saylor managed to score, and Reid State grabbed the ball and threw it back into play. Kyra willed her girls to run their press. When they ran it the way they were supposed to—which was rare—it was impenetrable. She'd spent hours upon hours perfecting it. She wasn't recycling something her high school coach had used, and it wasn't some press she'd found on YouTube.

No, this was a defense she herself had crafted.

And it worked.

When they ran it.

They didn't run it this time.

"Vicki!" Kyra screamed. "You have to cut off the sideline! What is wrong with you?" She felt like pulling her hair out, but if she did that every time she felt like it, she'd have been bald long ago.

Vicki's head dropped like a wilted flower.

"Pick your head up!" Kyra hollered. "Stop sulking!" She looked at her bench, which was full. Full of people who wouldn't cut off the sideline either. She turned her attention back to the floor in time to see Saylor score again.

Good. *Run the press this time.*

They did. Saylor intercepted a pass and went in for a layup.

Kyra didn't need to look at the clock to know that they'd tied the game, but she couldn't help it. As her eyes swung toward the small, round, red bulbs, they swept over that same man in the bleachers who was often looking at her.

Unlike the others, he didn't glare at her like she was a villain or stare at her like she was the bearded lady at the fair.

He looked at her the way a man stares at a woman when he thinks he won't get caught.

Of course, she kept catching him. So he wasn't very good at it.

Meghan's uncle, apparently, though he didn't look old enough to be a college athlete's uncle. He was cute, but she could tell from across the gym that he wasn't her type. He was wearing a flannel shirt, for starters.

Second, a man who was her type wouldn't have the time to go to all his niece's home games. Especially when she didn't even play.

Saylor stole the ball again and headed for the hoop. Good girl. It was a good thing Kyra had recruited her. No way that girl would have chosen Fort George if Kyra hadn't convinced her.

Up by two.

Kyra forced herself to breathe and sneaked another peek at the clock.

Less than a minute.

Way too close for comfort.

Saylor needed to do it again.

But not this time.

Again Vicki was too lazy to cut off the sideline, and Reid State broke Kyra's press. Well, not quite. Reid State had broken her team's sorry imitation of her press. No way could they have broken it if her girls had run it the way they were supposed to.

Reid State's best player drove toward the hoop, and Saylor set herself up for the charge. Both girls fell into a heap of limbs as the whistle pierced the rumble of the crowd. It seemed the whole crowd held their breath—Kyra certainly wasn't breathing.

The ref put his hands on his hips.

Blocking foul.

Kyra's stomach turned over as her chest tightened with panic. *No, God, not like this. Don't let us lose to Reid State. Not now.* They weren't even halfway into their season yet, but last year had given them a reputation to live up to. People were expecting her to take them to the national playoffs, but they couldn't get there without another conference title, and that conference title was going to be a lot harder to get if they didn't go into the playoffs with a good seed.

Reid State's foul shot bounced off the rim, and Vicki got the rebound. She held onto it while the clock ran out. When the buzzer sounded, Kyra looked at the clock again, just to make sure.

They had squeaked by.

But she couldn't let it be so close next time.

Chapter 2

You can do this, Brad Foster told himself, trying to coax his feet across the gym.

He'd been trying to get up the nerve to ask this woman out since last season. Now Meghan had finally given him his opening.

But first, he had to get his feet to move.

Come on left foot. Just one step. It moved. Excellent. That had been a close one. Now, the right foot. Even better. He was moving across the gym. And none too soon. The crowd was thinning out. Soon Coach Kyra would disappear like she always did.

He took a big breath. She was just a woman. This wasn't that big of a deal. Normal men asked out beautiful woman all the time. It was sort of the point of being a man. Just because he hadn't done it in a few years didn't mean it was an extraordinary thing to do. And just because she was beautiful didn't mean she was supernatural or superhuman. She was still just a woman.

And this particular beautiful woman was none too popular in town. Maybe she'd be glad to have a friend. Of course, he wanted to try for more than friendship, but he was happy to start there.

Oh no. She'd seen him coming.

Oh good. She wasn't running away.

He forced a smile, worried it was too big, and tried to tone it down a little. "Hi."

She didn't say anything, but she stared at him expectantly.

"Meghan tells me you're having some trouble with your stats software. Thought I might be able to help."

She stared at him as if he'd spoken a different language.

He tried to think of a way to make his offer clearer. Had Meghan messed up? Was there no broken software? If not, then he was looking like a fool.

"It's just a spreadsheet," she finally said. "I broke it."

That would be even easier. But he didn't want to make her feel stupid. "I know my way around Excel too, if you'd like me to take a look."

Again she hesitated.

"Or not." He started to back away. "I just wanted to offer."

"No, no," she said quickly.

Was that a bit of pink in her cheeks? It was hard to tell beneath the makeup. "Can you give me a minute? I need to talk to the girls. And then I can show you."

Show him? Even better. He'd expected that she would email it to him. "Sure. Of course."

"Great. Thanks." She stiffly walked away, and he wondered where he was supposed to wait for her. He didn't know where her office was. So he stood where he was and watched the gym empty out.

When someone started shutting the lights off, he wondered if he was a bigger idiot than he'd thought. Had she forgotten about him? Surely she hadn't intentionally left him standing out here alone?

Should he leave? Was he really going to stand there in the dark?

And then she appeared, her graceful outline barely visible among the shadows.

Good grief, she was beautiful.

But there was more than that, wasn't there? If there wasn't, that would make him a shallow twit.

"Sorry about that," she said, sounding more relaxed then he'd ever heard her. "Come on back." She vanished through a doorway, and he hurried to catch up—through the doorway into a narrow, carpeted hallway and up a small set of stairs to another hallway. Offices sprang off this corridor on both sides. He hadn't known this hidden annex of offices was back here. Of course, if he were her, he wouldn't want the Joe Shmoes of the world knowing where his office was either.

And then he was inside the inner sanctum. She'd flicked on a desk lamp that cast a warm orange glow over the room. Her curtains were blue and gold—Fort George school colors. A giant bookshelf lined one wall. The shelves were loaded with books, and more than a dozen trophies decorated the top of the bookshelf.

She followed his eyes.

"That's a lot of books," he said stupidly.

"I learn a lot from reading about other coaches." She sounded a touch defensive.

"That's a lot of trophies."

Her eyes slid to the well-organized shelf. "There's been a lot of basketball." Her eyes lingered on the trophies and then went back to his. "Unfortunately, I better remember the ones I didn't win than those I did."

This didn't surprise him. He loved that she was talking to him like this, being so open. Her voice was lovely when she wasn't screaming. He tried to think of a way to keep the small talk rolling while she stared at him expectantly.

Suddenly she jumped. "Sorry. The spreadsheet." She sat in her chair and wiggled the mouse. Her leg bounced up and down as she waited for her computer to wake up.

"You've got a good team this year," he said awkwardly.

She didn't look up. "They've got potential." She double clicked the mouse and popped up out of her chair. "Here you go."

He went around the desk, nervous to be so close to her. When he sat in her chair, she leaned on her desk, and her smell washed over him.

Flowers. But not the cloying kind. More like a subtle hint. Fresh, soft, gentle.

Wild roses.

She pointed at the screen. "So I have each girls' totals ..." She reached for the mouse, and her hand brushed his. "Oh, sorry."

"No, no," he said too quickly. "You're good."

She clicked to another sheet. "And I want their totals to all appear on the same page, and they used to."

She straightened, and he wished she hadn't. Right away he had an idea what the problem was, but he considered pretending not to know so he could hang out with her longer.

"Are you all set in here?" She stepped away. "I have to go lock some doors."

So much for lingering. "I am all set, but I'm guessing this won't take long if you want to hang on a sec."

She stopped edging away. "Oh. Okay."

He clicked into a cell and then another. "Just need to tweak your formula here." He shifted in the chair, suddenly uncomfortable beneath her gaze. Good grief, what was he sitting on, an 1800s church pew? He looked down at the chair and then up at her. "Would you like me to organize a fundraiser to get you a new chair?"

She laughed, and it was the most beautiful sound he'd ever heard. It sort of floated on the air like the last notes of a song he loved but hadn't heard in a long time.

"No thank you. I think that one is good for my posture."

Of course she did.

"For health reasons, not vanity," she specified, but he wasn't sure he believed her. She didn't sound very confident in her defense.

He tapped some keys and then clicked to the front page to see if the data had copied over. It had not. Of course. He was hardly looking at the screen he was so distracted by her. He went back and tried again.

Bingo.

"Okay, I fixed one of the girls." Wait, should he call them girls? He knew Meghan wanted to be considered a woman. But some of them were only eighteen. He was thirty. It felt creepy calling them women. "I'm assuming you want me to copy the correction to each of the sheets?"

She came closer. "Yes, please. Wow, it was that simple? I must be an idiot."

"No, not at all," he said quickly. "I'm just a computer nerd. I actually like spreadsheets." *Oh my salt, how embarrassing.* "Weird, I know."

She giggled. "How does someone like spreadsheets?"

He stopped himself from saying, "How does someone like foul shots?" He clicked through the sheets, pasting the new formula into each one. Wow, this was a lot of data. "You sure do keep a lot of stats."

"Yes, I make a lot of decisions based on numbers."

He looked up. "Like *Money Ball*?"

She laughed again. "Kind of, yeah."

"I like that movie." This would be a great segue into asking her to the movies.

"I remember liking it too, but I haven't seen it in a long time. I haven't had time to watch a movie in years."

Okay, maybe not a good segue. He finished his assignment and stood. He was going to go for it anyway. "You should make time."

"Huh?"

"For a movie. You should make time. How about this Friday?" He knew they didn't have a game that night.

She stared at him dumbly, and he realized she was the exact same height as him. She'd looked smaller out on the floor, when he was up in the bleachers. He wasn't a short man. Which meant she was a tall woman. He resisted the urge to check if she was wearing heels.

Would be a pretty awkward time to look at her feet.

"Uh ..." she tried.

Uh oh, he had her tongue tied. He tried to convince himself that this was a good thing. She was so smitten, she couldn't speak.

But he wasn't convinced.

"That's kind of you, but I don't even know you."

"Oh, you're right. We should have dinner first." Good one, he silently praised himself. Quick on his feet.

She did smile, but her guard was definitely up. "What's your name?"

He laughed awkwardly. "You know what? I'm sorry, I'm kind of bad at this. I'm Brad Foster, Meghan's cousin."

"Cousin? I thought she'd said you were her uncle."

He exhaled. He wanted to explain without getting too deep and dark. "Her father was my first cousin, and we were close, so she used to call me uncle when she was little. Then when he passed away, I tried to be there for her, and the name sort of stuck. But no, I'm not her uncle really. Only a cousin. Or a second cousin. Or a first cousin once removed." *Oh God, please strike me dumb right now.* "Sorry, I'm not sure how that cousin labeling works."

"I don't know how that works either. I don't have a big family, so never bothered to figure it out." Her expression had softened. "But that is really amazing. So good of you to try to step in like that. Where do you work?"

The abruptness of subject change made him fumble for an answer to her simple question. "Uh ... Freedom Academy."

"The Christian school?" She looked horrified.

He grinned broadly. "Yeah, but don't worry, I'm one of those cool Christians." He didn't know what that meant, exactly, but he hoped it would ease her fear of being thumped with a Bible.

She didn't move, but he could feel her backing away, nonetheless. "Oh no, no, I'm a Christian too. But ... when you said you were a computer nerd, I figured you worked in IT."

"I do. I'm the IT guy at Freedom. And I teach the computer classes."

The horror stayed firmly on her face. He swallowed nervously. Well, at least she wasn't horrified by Jesus. Score one point. But she was horrified by his job. Take one point away.

"Cool." She straightened. "I am really glad to meet you, and I am really grateful to you for fixing my spreadsheet, but it's probably not a good idea to date a relative of one of my girls."

Oh good. She'd called them girls too. "That rule totally works for me. I'll tell Meghan to quit the team."

She didn't laugh.

"Just a joke."

"Oh." She smiled. "Well, thank you for your time and expertise." She was verbally ushering him out of her office. It made sense. It was the middle of the night. And she was turning down his offer of dinner and a movie. This made sense too. She was a beautiful woman. She probably had lots of suitors. At least she'd been polite about it.

On his way out, she said, "You know, Fort George is always looking for IT personnel."

He stopped and faced her.

"If you would be interested in a job."

Weird. Had he given her the impression that he didn't like his job? "Thanks, but I'm happy where I am."

"Oh, okay," she said quickly. She stepped into the hallway, pulling the door shut behind her. "Thanks again." She passed him and started down the hallway, and he followed.

When she picked up speed, he didn't try to keep up. He veered off toward the door, and she didn't give him another look.

He'd done it. He'd asked her out. She'd said no, maybe because he was a high school teacher, but whatever. It was all good. Now he could stop pining after her and find someone else to admire. This was a good thing. Better than not knowing. And besides, if she was the type of woman who would judge him for what he chose to do for a job, then he didn't want to go out with her anyway.

Chapter 3

Kyra traveled the inside perimeter of the field house, checking the outside doors one at a time, making sure they were each locked. They had security staff who were supposed to do this, but last year someone had still managed to get in and steal some stuff—they hadn't been particularly talented thieves as they'd only made off with a pair of twenty-pound dumbbells, a large bag of Wiffle Balls, and one ancient, broken computer from an unlocked storage closet—but still, she didn't want them to get another shot at it. So she'd been checking the doors ever since.

She was trying to calm herself down again. She had only just gotten her heart to stop racing from the game when Meghan's uncle ... no, cousin, had asked her out.

That had certainly come out of left field. He didn't even know her.

That was probably *why* he'd asked her out. He probably wouldn't have if he knew her better. Not that she was a monster or anything. She was attractive and worked to stay fit, but still, any man who had ever shown interest in her had quickly lost interest when they found out she had no intention of partying or sleeping around. Even the few Christian men she'd gone out with had proved themselves to be more a fan of Genesis

1:28 than Hebrews 13:4. The "be fruitful and multiply" part without the "be faithful" part.

An uninvited small voice in her head suggested that Brad might not be like that.

Brad.

What kind of a name was Brad? Talk about a generic, all-American, nondescript name. *Brad.* Like Bill. Or Ted. She laughed alone in the darkness.

He'd made her laugh. That had been cool. She didn't laugh much. And now she was still laughing at him long after he'd given up on her and gone home. Of course, now she was laughing at his name not his jokes, but still, he deserved the credit.

Laughing was fun.

She enjoyed laughing.

And it was a healthy thing to do.

She should do it more often.

She knew she took life too seriously sometimes, but life *was* serious. And it was short. She didn't have time or energy for things that didn't matter.

She tried to make herself stop thinking about him, about his smile, about how quickly he had solved her problem. He must be pretty smart. But she couldn't be dating some IT drop out. Even if he was cute and clever. Even if he did have such a big heart that he had taken his young cousin under his wing and now went to all of her home games—even though she never got off the bench.

Kyra shook her head and went back to her office to get her coat and bags. Maybe she should put Meghan into a game soon. Next time they had a big lead, she would do that. Of course, the way her team had played tonight, they might not have a big lead again for a long time. She shut her office door behind her and locked it.

Brad was nice. Sure. Cute. Sure. But he was headed nowhere in life, and she couldn't let herself be slowed down. Besides, she wasn't going to be in Maine much longer anyway. She shouldn't be getting attached and tied down to distractions, especially not to a distraction who could likely do damage to her reputation.

She could hear the critics now: *Did you hear? Young, inexperienced coach dating church IT guy.* Nope. That wasn't going to happen. She already had enough problems.

Chapter 4

B rad saw Cindy Harrington coming down the busy church hallway and ducked into the library. He pressed himself against the wall, closed his eyes, and held his breath.

Through his eyelids, he saw the light come on.

He opened one eye to see Cindy standing in the doorway smiling at him.

"Are you looking for something to read?"

He didn't know if she was kidding. Was he looking for a book in the dark? With his eyes closed? Of course not. But he also didn't want her to know that he was avoiding her.

Her eyes scanned the paltrily appointed shelves. "Are you into Amish romance?"

Amish what? His eyes followed hers, and sure enough, the shelves were dominated by bonnets and aprons. Dozens of Amish books followed by the arrestingly colorful spines of the Left Behind series and two dusty copies of Hal Lindsay's *Late Great Planet Earth.* Brad wasn't much of a reader, and even he could tell this library sorely needed an update. "Huh. I didn't know there was such a thing as Amish romance."

"Of course there is, silly. Where do you think all the Amish babies come from?"

He laughed nervously. He wasn't comfortable with mischievous humor coming from Cindy Harrington. She was one of those perfect Christians.

The perfect Christian folded her arms over her chest. "So, tell me why you're hiding from me in the church library."

He sighed. "I wasn't hiding."

She raised an eyebrow.

"Okay, maybe I was, a little, but it's not an insult. I just knew what you were going to say if you saw me."

"What was I going to say?"

"You were going to ask me if I've asked Kyra out yet—"

"Well, have you?"

"And I'm not in the mood to talk about it." He was *never* in the mood to talk about his love life, or lack thereof, with Cindy, but he'd spilled the beans about his basketball crush so that Cindy would stop trying to fix him up with the church's flutist.

"She said no?" She looked appalled, which instantly made him feel better about the whole thing.

He nodded.

"Good. You can go out with Samantha, then."

Samantha. The flutist. No, he didn't want to go out with Samantha. He had nothing against flutes, per se, but he just didn't feel any spark with her. "I think I need a break from the dating scene," he tried.

"A break? You can't take a break from something you're not doing! Come on, give Samantha a try. Tell you what, I'll invite a bunch of people over to my house for dinner, and I'll make sure you and Samantha make the guest list."

"Cindy, is Samantha even interested in me?" He was confident that she wasn't. She never even looked at him.

"She is. She might not know it yet, but she is."

He gave a dirty look.

She playfully jabbed him in the shoulder. "Come on. Trust me. I know what I'm doing."

"Cindy, I love you, but you need to come up with a new hobby."

She narrowed her eyes. "I've never thought that coach was the woman for you, and I have a sense about these things. I hadn't heard a good word about her, and I've been listening. And she's just proven them all correct by turning you down."

"No ..." He couldn't help but feel defensive of Kyra. "She doesn't have it easy. Her every move is under a microscope, and she doesn't want to go out with one of her athlete's relatives."

"Is that what she said?"

"Yes," he said, thankful that it was. It hadn't been true when she'd said it, but she had said it.

"Fine then. I'll find someone else for Samantha." Cindy stepped closer and softened her voice. "But really, Brad. You are a great guy with a lot to offer. Don't let yourself get hung up on someone who's not worth it. I don't want you to get hurt."

He managed to not roll his eyes. "I'm a big boy, Cindy. I can take care of myself, thank you."

"I know that." She took a step back. "I didn't mean to suggest otherwise." She headed for the door. "Have a good service."

Oh yeah, he had to get moving. The service was going to start. He followed her out of the tiny library and toward the sanctuary.

He had spoken the truth. He was a big boy, and he could take care of himself. And he wasn't going to get hurt because Kyra wouldn't get close enough to him to do any damage.

But he almost wished she would.

January 10

Dear Frank,

Great news!

That basketball coach turned down Brad Foster! Sorry, but that is cheering me up after that dreary new years I just suffered through. I don't mean to be too hard on her, but she's so ... harsh, I think might be the word. And Brad is so gentle and easygoing. I just can't see it working. I think she might squish him like a bug under the heel of her fancy boot.

Okay, I feel like you'd be annoyed by now, so we can talk about something else.

Stan is in the hospital, and they are telling Paula that there's only about a twenty percent chance he'll be coming home. I hate it when they put numbers like that on it. So she's going crazy with worry. I'm trying to help, but there's not much to do but pray. If we do lose him, then I'll be sure to be of some hands-on worth. I promise. I hope it doesn't come to that, but if it does, it will be nice to know you've got another hunting buddy up there with you. Of course, they probably don't have hunting in heaven, but I'm sure you men will find some way to enjoy your bliss.

I love you, Frank. When I see other women going through what I had to go through, it brings losing you back to the forefront. And I hate it. You *might think this matchmaking is silly, but it sure does distract me from my grief. So there. Just try to stop me! Ha!*

Love you bunches,
Cindy

Chapter 5

When Kyra walked into the locker room, the girls fell silent. This was unusual and made her stop and look up. Usually, she had to beg them to be quiet and listen. But now the place was as quiet as a tomb. Yet none of them were looking at her.

A chill danced across her shoulders. They'd been talking about her. That much was clear. But it was more than that. "What's going on?"

"Nothing." Madison sat down on the bench and gave her a cryptically plastic smile. "Nothing at all."

Kyra's eyes slid to Meghan, but she was busy studying the floor. She wasn't particularly close to Meghan or to any of them, but Meghan was always respectful.

"Okay then." She took a big breath and tried to act unshaken, when she was practically trembling. She picked up a marker from the white-board railing. "Let's play some basketball then because Teelock's win streak is over as of tonight." She turned to the board, and someone snickered behind her. She whirled around to see Avery with her hand over her mouth.

"Do you have something to say, Avery?"

Avery raised her eyes to meet Kyra's. There was a boldness in them Kyra hadn't seen before. Avery wasn't usually this confident. But it was clear that right now Avery knew something that Kyra didn't know.

Something was very wrong.

"So you're courageous enough to sneak and speak behind my back, but not courageous enough to say something to my face?"

Avery still wore the smug grin. It didn't make sense. She was a junior, a terrible basketball player by all accounts. She had nothing to be smug about.

Kyra set the marker down and pointed to the hallway. "Outside." She started toward the door, but Avery didn't move. She didn't even stand up.

Kyra shook with anger. Whatever this was, she could run it out of them tomorrow, but right now they had a game to play. She didn't have time for this.

"Get out in that hallway now, or you can forget about sitting on my bench tonight."

"Don't," a meek voice piped up from her left.

Kyra spun that way to see Meghan looking at her, her eyes wide with worry.

So whatever it was, Meghan knew about it too. And the look she was giving Kyra right now—like silently handing her a ten-ton weight. Clearly, Meghan was trying to help her, but Kyra couldn't quite translate her facial expression into useful information. And no matter what Meghan was trying to tell her, Kyra couldn't let Avery get away with what she was doing.

Kyra looked at Avery, the junior she'd inherited last season. Sure, she could have cut her at tryouts, but she hadn't had the heart to cut a girl who'd been on the team the year before. And so she'd put her on the roster.

And now she was regretting it.

"Avery, if you decide to grace the gym with your presence tonight, you can do so from the bleachers on the other side."

The smug look slid off her face, replaced by something worse—pure vitriol.

Kyra turned to the rest of her team. "Now, for the rest of you. Let's go beat Teelock." She looked at the whiteboard and then at her watch. She was out of time. "Let's go warm up." She stepped out of the way and watched them leave.

Avery didn't move.

Meghan stood up but didn't leave.

Soon it was the three of them standing there in a tense triangle.

"What are you waiting for?" Avery asked Meghan, her words clipped with hatred. This was weird. Kyra was pretty sure these two were friends. Or at least friendly. They were both local girls.

"Waiting for you," Meghan said quickly, lightly.

"Oh." Avery gave Kyra another glare and then headed for the door.

Meghan fell in behind her and whispered, "I thought you wouldn't want to be alone with her."

"Oh. Right," Avery said.

Kyra stood still and watched the door shut behind them.

Meghan had whispered those words, but she'd said them loudly enough for Kyra to hear them. She wasn't stupid. She knew how to gauge a whisper. So she'd meant for Kyra to hear that. But why? What had it even meant? Why wouldn't Avery want to be alone with her? She was a tough coach, but she wasn't abusive.

None of it made sense, and Kyra's belly swam with a fear she tried to tamp down.

Just do the next thing, she told herself. It was her mantra whenever she was overwhelmed. The next thing was leaving the locker room, so she did that. Then she had to go up the stairs.

The sound of the crowd made her sick with apprehension.

She stepped into the gym as the first notes of the warmup music blared from the speakers.

She swung her eyes over the crowd, looking for clues as to what was happening, but everything looked ordinary.

Her eyes fell on Brad Foster, who, for once, was not looking at her. She couldn't blame him. She'd shot him down. Good for him, not looking at her. Yet the sight of him brought a measure of steadiness.

Like she was in a raft adrift in rough waters, and he was land in sight.

She took a breath and held her chin up as she walked the baseline and then followed the sideline to her bench.

Her feet stopped in her usual spot, and she spun to watch her girls warm up.

Wait.

Avery was out there.

After Kyra had told her not to be. Kyra was hot with anger, but she couldn't exactly march out onto the floor and grab the girl. Instead, she followed the sideline to that end of the gym and tried to sound calm and collected as she called the wannabe athlete's name.

Predictably, Avery ignored her.

She said her name again, louder this time. She glanced up to see some of the fans staring at her. What a pickle she was in. She either had to make a scene or let her player win the standoff.

So she had to make a scene.

She opened her mouth to holler again. One more time and then she'd have to go out onto the floor. But Meghan trotted over to her, looking pale.

"Coach, please, don't."

Kyra stared at Meghan. "Excuse me?" If Kyra had seen an ounce of sass in Meghan's demeanor, she might have blown a fuse, but all she saw was fear. "What is it, Meghan?"

"Just please." She backed up a step. "Let her play. It's better for you." She kept backing up as she spoke, leaving Kyra even more bewildered.

It killed Kyra to give in, but she was too scared not to. As she turned back to her bench, she heard Saylor say, "What did you just say to her?" in a voice that was pure bully.

Kyra couldn't hear Meghan's response, but it was not lost on her that Meghan had taken a risk in telling her to throw in the towel.

When Kyra got back to her bench, Coach Weiger was there. "Hey, do you know what's going on?" Kyra asked.

"What do you mean?"

"The girls are acting weird."

"They're always weird."

"No, not like that. Like something's going on, and I don't know about it. Like some kind of conspiracy."

Tamara snorted. "A conspiracy?"

For a second, Kyra hated her assistant and let the matter drop. Even if she cared enough to be a help, she probably wouldn't know anything. So Kyra stood there watching her girls warm up, trying to stay calm, trying not to let her imagination run wild with all the things those girls might conspire about.

Chapter 6

When Meghan ran over to the bench to take off her warmups, Kyra tried not to move her lips when she said, "Thank you."

Meghan didn't respond. She didn't even look at her.

Kyra glanced at Meghan's teammates and sure enough, Saylor and Madison were glaring at her. Still, Kyra cared more about knowing the secret than she did about protecting Meghan. She turned her back on the other players and looked at Meghan. "Please tell me what's going on."

Meghan busied herself with folding her shirt and mumbled, "I can't." But then as she turned to trot back onto the floor, she passed unnecessarily close to Kyra and quickly said, "But you really should go out with my uncle."

What? What did that have to do with anything?

Kyra watched her go, and Meghan turned around to add. "Trust me. Go tonight."

"What was that all about?" Tamara asked, coming alongside her.

"No idea. I told you. Something's wrong." Kyra's eyes slid to Brad. He still wasn't looking at her. How was she supposed to go out with him tonight? And what did he have to do with anything? As she stared at him, she realized an unusual percentage of the fans were looking at her now.

And part of the picture came into view. Not enough of the picture so she could guess what was going on. Not enough so she could make a plan, figure out how deal with it. But enough to know that there was a lie afoot.

Someone had said something about her, and it wasn't true.

She knew it wasn't true because her record was flawless. She didn't make mistakes. She didn't do stupid things. She didn't give people anything to gossip about.

Meghan didn't care about her love life. She probably didn't care about Brad's either. But she was trying to hand Kyra a cover story.

Kyra looked at the clock. Oh no. Was that enough time? She started toward the baseline, her dress shoes making a quick, uncomfortably loud clap-clap on the hardwood. She rounded the corner and more eyes turned toward her.

She could feel their disgust.

God, please fix this. Whatever it is. Protect me. "Brad?" she called up into the bleachers. She forced a smile. Under other circumstances, his shock would have made her laugh. But now it only brought comfort. Whatever the lie was, she didn't think he'd heard it. Yet. "Would you mind coming back and helping me with that computer problem again?"

His eyes grew even wider. "Now?"

She nodded quickly. "If you wouldn't mind." She was starting to feel faint. She forced herself to take a breath.

"Of course." He stood and extricated himself from the bleachers.

Mumbles followed his descent, but she couldn't make out any words.

She forced another smile at him. "Sorry, we have to hurry." She started back toward the baseline, hoping he would follow.

Not only did he follow, but he caught up. "What's wrong?" The genuineness of his concern was sweet. He sounded so kind, just like he'd sounded last week when he'd asked her out. How she wished she'd taken him up on his offer.

She didn't answer him, just ran up the steps into the office annex. Then she turned and faced him. "I can't even imagine how bizarre this must seem, but I have to ask." She took a quick break for a quick breath, and the buzzer sounded in the gym. "Can we go on that date tonight?"

His concern turned into amusement.

She tapped her toe, waiting for her answer.

"Yeah ... of course."

Gratitude washed over her. "Great. Thank you so much." She leaned in and gave him a quick peck on the cheek and then practically ran to the gym. That might have been overly familiar, she thought on her way, but she'd been so, so grateful that he'd said yes.

Her girls were already at the bench, half of them looking at her with bizarre, playful expressions. The other half wouldn't meet her eyes.

Meghan was watching her cousin come out of the annex.

Kyra clapped her hands together. "Line up." She stood behind her athletes as the national anthem began to play. Not for the first time, she bemoaned what a terrible rendition they used. She should really find them a newer, classier version.

She stared at the flag and thought about the game in front of her. *Do the next thing, Kyra.* That was win the game. Then she would go out with the high school computer teacher.

It was so nice of him to save her like that.

Now she just had to figure out what he was saving her from.

Chapter 7

B rad sat in the bleachers in a daze. What on earth had just happened? He wanted to believe that the woman had simply changed her mind and asked him out. That would be a neat, sweet story they could one day tell cute little grandkids.

But that's not what had happened.

Kyra had been scared of something. It was hard to imagine something that she could be scared of in a packed gym, and it was even harder to imagine that she would consider *him* a protector. He was scared of spiders, for crying out loud. And mayonnaise. That last one was irrational, he knew, but the fear persisted. His parents claimed there was no rhyme nor reason, but he was sure he'd suffered some condiment-induced trauma as a child.

Kyra Carter probably didn't need him to protect her from mayonnaise.

But whatever it was, he would do his best to step into the role. He might get beaten up, bitten by an arachnid, or slathered in white goo, but he would give it the old college try.

But where was he going to take her? The game wouldn't be over until nine. He searched on his phone for restaurants that would be open that late. There were two: Ecstatic Enchilada; or House of Salsa. He put his phone to sleep and shoved it into his pocket. Mexican it was, then.

He turned his focus to the game, the mechanisms of which made him wonder if someone had slipped him some hallucinogenic drug.

First, the beautiful woman who had recently rejected him had panic-asked him out.

And now her team was playing weird.

But not quite weird enough that he could put a finger on it. They hadn't turned into the Washington Generals or anything, but something was off.

For starters, point guard Saylor was being a total ball hog. This was unusual and made stranger by the appearance that her teammates weren't upset by it. Even weirder, Kyra wasn't yelling at her to pass the ball. And it wasn't like Saylor was hitting every shot. No, she wasn't even playing well. *And* she was laughing a lot—miss another shot and then laugh it off—giving the appearance that she was having great fun, but even to Brad's untrained eye, it looked as though she was acting.

His eyes drifted back to Kyra. She'd sat down. She never sat down. And she was being quiet. She was mostly expressionless, but he could feel her stress from across the court.

Maybe she wasn't feeling well.

No, sick people didn't panic-ask someone out.

Saylor took yet another three-point shot, missed by a mile, and then laughed as none of her teammates tried to get the rebound. This was the sort of thing that would have made the Kyra of yesterday blow her top. Maybe he didn't know her as well as he thought he did. Coach Weiger, her assistant, stood up and hollered at Saylor to run the offense.

Kyra reached up, gently grabbed her assistant's elbow, and slowly pulled her down to the bench. Weiger looked stunned. Whatever was going on, she wasn't privy to it.

Over the next several minutes, Weiger tried again and again to right the ship, and again and again Kyra subtly discouraged that. Apparently Kyra wanted to let the girls control this game.

Whether this was a good idea was questionable.

Voices around and behind Brad started to complain. The same voices that had spent the season complaining about how Kyra hollered too much were now saying she wasn't hollering enough. For weeks they'd been saying that she was too focused on winning, and now they were terrified she was going to let them lose.

Brad was a little worried about that himself. Whatever was going on with her, whatever she was afraid of, he didn't think losing a game would help. Of course, this wasn't *Friday Night Lights*. If this Division III women's team lost a game, no one was going to pepper the coach's lawn with real estate signs.

But still.

He wished she'd look at him, so he could offer her a comforting smile. But her eyes were focused on the ball. They followed it up and down the court and went nowhere else. She didn't put subs in. She didn't call time outs. She didn't do anything but sit there. She didn't even look at the score clock, which she usually did fifteen times a minute.

Brad looked at the score clock now and winced. They were down by two. Were they really going to lose this game? Was Kyra going to let that happen?

Chapter 8

Kyra didn't want to get into a vehicle with Brad Foster. She hardly knew him. Then she remembered that he was a computer teacher at a Christian school. How dangerous could he be? Besides, if someone saw them in the vehicle together, that would be good.

She snapped her buckle into place and tried to calm her breathing.

"So that was weird," Brad said. He'd been quiet on the way to his car.

Weird was the right adjective, for sure, but she didn't know which noun he was referencing. "What was weird?"

He started driving. "Were you doing some sort of experiment?"

She still didn't understand.

He chuckled uncomfortably. "I thought maybe you were going to let them lose to prove to them that they need you."

If only it were that simple. His was a ridiculous theory, which made her wonder what the rest of the spectators had thought. She hadn't been thinking about them at all. Maybe she should have. She'd spent the forty minutes of basketball trying to figure out what on earth was going on.

She'd hoped that getting out onto the court would have brought things back to normal, but that's not what had happened. Half of her girls acted smug and amused, and half of them acted scared.

None of them had told her what had happened. But something had certainly happened.

"I'm sorry," Brad said gently. "I didn't mean to be critical. I was just being nosy. You don't have to tell me any—"

"No, no. I don't mind you asking. I'm just a little ... overwhelmed." She was also exhausted. Much too exhausted to try to execute any sort of ruse. "Look, I don't know you that well, but I'm hoping you can't be evil if you choose to teach computer at a Christian school."

He chuckled.

"You *did* choose that, right? You're not there because no one else would hire you?"

He raised an eyebrow. "Now who's being nosy?"

She laughed and felt some of the weight lift.

"Yes, I work there on purpose."

"Oh good. And you're not evil?"

"No, I am not evil."

She took a big breath. "Good. Because I don't really have the energy for anything other than honesty, and the truth is, I think I ..." Her voice broke, and she stopped talking to try to stave off tears. Goodness, when had she gotten so tired?

"Take your time."

"Thank you," she whispered.

He reached across in front of her and opened the glove box, pulled out a small package of tissues, and then pressed them into her sweaty palm. Unexpectedly, his touch sent a chill up her arm.

"Thank you," she said again. She wasn't crying yet, but the dam was cracking.

"How do you feel about Mexican food?"

She smiled, grateful for his redirect. "I love it far more than I should."

"Good." He turned on his blinker. "Because the only restaurants still open in Hartport serve burritos."

Hartport. Small-town, coastal Maine. It was still hard to believe she'd ended up here. Her first visit and her interview had been deceiving. It had seemed so quaint, so picturesque, so homey.

And in July, if you were a tourist, that's exactly what Hartport was.

That's not what it was in January. In January, the wind came off the water like it was trying to kill you. Air stabbed into your lungs like jagged icicles, and if you were outside for more than a minute, the skin on your face started to hurt. The only answer to this was high-collared coats that completely ruined foundation and lip gloss.

She hated winter. She almost hated Hartport, especially after tonight.

He pulled into the parking lot of a brightly colored building.

"House of Salsa," she read the sign aloud. "Cute."

He turned the engine off and twisted his upper body to face her, resting his hand on the back of her seat. "We don't have to go in if you're not up for it. I can go get takeout and we can eat in the car."

It was a little cold for that.

He read her mind. "I'll keep the engine running so that we don't freeze to death with refried beans on our lips."

She laughed again and felt herself relax some more. His plan was sound, but she wanted to be seen with him in public. She didn't know how that could help, but she had a feeling. "No, no, let's go in."

"Okay, then." He got out of the car, and she did the same, meeting him in front of the hood. Suddenly she was nervous. She was actually on a date. She hadn't meant for this to happen. She forced a smile and then headed for the door.

He followed but jumped in front of her to open it for her. A voice in her head told her to be offended by this, but the gesture made her belly warm.

A friendly host seated them and gave them menus. She looked around the well-decorated room. Between the color scheme and the upbeat music, maybe the place could cheer her up.

Her eyes fell on Brad's, and she was suddenly self-conscious. This was a small table. He was sitting really close to her. He had a pretty good view. She leaned back in her seat, wishing he too would take some time to admire the color scheme.

He might have read her mind, or maybe he was just hungry, but he gave his attention to the menu.

She did the same, and as soon as she started reading the descriptions, her hunger roared to life. If the bright primary colors and the Latin music didn't do it, the food would. She could hardly wait for its sedative effect.

But once they'd ordered, they were back to staring at each other. She'd started a sentence in the car and never finished it. Maybe she should do that now. Otherwise, he was afraid to ask any questions, apparently.

"So, something bad has happened. Or is happening. Or is about to happen." She paused for a breath, but it was hard to do, her chest was so tight. "I don't know what it is. But something happened with the girls. They're all acting strange. Rebellious and smug. I think they know something that I don't know." She made herself look at him, and his eyes were full of tender concern. "And if they know something I don't know, and they're smug about it, then that can't be good. Not for me, anyway."

Chapter 9

*O*h my salt, is she beautiful. Even in obvious distress, Kyra Carter was a knockout. Brad wanted to go to her side of the booth, wrap his arms around her, and tell her to quit her job. She was an amazing coach. She could work anywhere.

But he didn't, of course.

"I think I'm in trouble," she said softly, and her eyes welled up. She tipped her head up and blinked rapidly.

He didn't know what to say.

"I think I'm about to be fired."

"Fired?" That was a little extreme. "I highly doubt they will fire the woman who gave them their first conference championship."

She shook her head slowly. "You didn't see the arrogance on their faces."

Actually, he had. He took out his phone. "I'll ask Meghan."

Her hand shot up from her lap and out toward him, landing over his phone and hand. Her fingertips were soft and warm. "Don't," she said strongly. Then she softened her voice. "Please."

"Why not?"

She shook her head as if she wasn't quite sure what to say.

"I don't have to tell her that you're the one who's asking. She doesn't even know that I've talked to you."

"Yes, she does." Her hand slid away, which was a bit of a bummer. "She knows we were going out tonight." It seemed there was more she had to say about that, but she held back.

"Okay ..." he said slowly. He didn't understand her reservation. "But she's a good girl. If you're in trouble, she's not going to be celebrating." This was insane. They both sounded paranoid. "Kyra—"

Her head snapped toward him at the sound of her name, her dark eyes finding his. It was a bit unsettling.

"I don't think you're in trouble. Unless you've done something wrong that I don't know about?" He couldn't imagine what that might be. She was too worried about her image, her reputation, to do something stupid.

"I haven't done anything wrong. But that hasn't stopped people from accusing me of things."

"Like what?" he asked even though he had a pretty good idea.

She sighed and leaned her elbows on the table. "I'm too hard on the girls. I make them work too hard. I criticize them too much." She rolled her eyes. "These people are wrong of course, but if the right person complains, what's right and wrong goes out the window."

That was a pretty cynical way of looking at things. He leaned forward too. "Tell me something. How long have you been coaching?"

"Eight years."

He nodded. "And in all those seasons, have you ever gotten into trouble?"

"I've had parent complaints."

"Everyone gets parent complaints because everyone can't play little Susie as much as mom wants." He didn't know if this was true, but he thought it had to be. "But have you ever gotten into *trouble*? Like, written up, suspended, fired?"

She shook her head slowly back and forth, her eyes not leaving his.

He leaned back, feeling satisfied. "Well, there then. I doubt you're about to start now."

The fear didn't leave her eyes.

He so badly wanted to say, so what? So what if she got fired? God would still take care of her. She could still coach somewhere else, somewhere that wanted her. That was probably her problem anyway. She was too good of a coach for the likes of Fort George.

A man arrived with two giant plates. "Careful, they are hot," he said with an accent.

Brad thanked him.

"Can I get you anything else?"

"No, thank you."

"Could we please get some more tortilla chips?" Kyra asked.

The server looked at the full basket in the middle of their table. It hadn't been touched.

"Trust me. I'm really hungry."

He smiled, nodded, and spun away.

She grabbed the biggest chip from the basket, swirled it around in her enchilada sauce, and shoved the whole thing in her mouth. Brad couldn't believe it fit. As she crunched, she put her hand over her mouth. It was adorable. "Oh," she said with her mouth full. "That *is* a little hot."

Brad laughed and then, as much as he wanted to watch her eat, he wanted her to enjoy her meal and not feel self-conscious, so he focused on his own food.

They dined in a pleasant silence for several minutes. When the door opened behind them, she jerked around to look. Then she looked disappointed.

"Expecting someone?"

"No, no." She waved him off. "I barely know anyone in this town."

This was sad. She'd been here for over a year. "I could introduce you to some people if you like."

She gave him a dry look. "I don't think I'm going to be here long enough to make friends."

"Will you please trust me? You're not getting fired."

"No, no. That's not what I meant. Even if this whole thing amounts to nothing, Hartport isn't my final destination." And despite all the emotions she'd shown and all the chips she'd eaten, she managed to sound uppity.

His heart sank. Of course it wasn't. "Just a steppingstone, huh?"

She nodded, missing the criticism in his voice. "Something like that." She didn't look up from her food.

Well, at least she was enjoying her meal. And she seemed less panicky. He could understand this. Cheese had that effect on him too.

But as he ate, her words ate at him. She had no friends? What kind of a life was that? He had a zillion friends. Maybe he should share some of them with her. Not the good-looking ones, of course. He concentrated, trying to think of which ones were the good-looking ones.

"You look deep in thought."

He grinned, his cheeks growing warm. He wasn't about to admit he'd been evaluating the handsomeness of his male friends. "Do you go to church in town?"

She nodded. "Gretel Street."

Whoa. He hadn't been expecting that. He tried to hide his surprise, but he didn't need to. She was focused on her rice.

Of all the churches, he wouldn't have picked that one for her in a million years. Why had *she* picked that one?

"I've heard that church is a little ..." He tried to think of a polite word. "Strict." This wasn't the right word, but he couldn't think of a better one.

"They can be."

"Are they friendly?" He'd been hearing for years that the opposite was true.

She shrugged. "I don't know. They can be, I guess. I usually get there right before service starts so there's not much time for chit chat."

He sensed that this was by design.

"You're kind of famous around here. Surely someone has asked for your autograph by now."

She didn't laugh.

"That was a joke."

"Oh." Her mind was a million miles away. "Yeah, I don't think any of them even know what I do."

"Seriously?" People talked about her all over town.

She shrugged again and picked up another chip. She was halfway through the second basket now. She hadn't been kidding. "I get there on time. I leave when it's over. No one asks me where I work."

She didn't sound disappointed by this, but he was. "Do they ask you anything?"

She looked at him. "What do you mean?"

"I mean, do they know you at all?"

"Not really, I guess. But that's okay. Like I said, just passing through."

Chapter 10

Kyra had spent all day waiting for the phone to ring, waiting for a text message that told her to come to the athletic director's office, waiting for some explanation.

Crickets.

Had she imagined the whole thing? It was as if nothing had happened.

But when she stepped into the gym, her boss was sitting in a metal folding chair by the table. He gave her a big smile that seemed sincere. Still, what was he doing in her gym?

"Hi, Dave."

"Hi. How are things going?"

How was she supposed to answer that? She had no idea how things were going. But if something had happened and she didn't mention it, he might think she was trying to cover something up. "You know, things are a little weird, actually."

If this admission surprised him, he hid it well.

"I feel like there's something going on that I don't know about."

His smile faded. "You're a good coach, Kyra. And I've got your back." He waved his hand toward the door, where girls were filtering in. "Go ahead and do your job. Let me take care of the other stuff."

She studied him. He'd been the one to hire her. He'd always been good to her. But could she really trust him? Her heart wanted to. Her head thought it was reasonable. Her gut had doubts. Over the years she'd learned to trust her gut.

But her boss was right that the girls were coming in. She had to coach. So she gave him a small smile and turned toward her team.

"Just pretend I'm not here," he said behind her.

Yeah, right. Super easy to pretend the athletic director wasn't watching her coach a routine practice.

She took attendance and then watched closely as they ran through their warmups, looking for some clues. They were acting mostly normal, but they were quieter than usual.

She put them through the drills she'd planned, and Saylor was completely nonchalant. When they reviewed their motion offense, she took Saylor out and put in a sub.

"What?" Saylor cried, throwing her hands up into the air.

Kyra ignored her. She couldn't let her boss see her letting some young, arrogant athlete walk all over her, even if she was an out-of-state superstar that Kyra had worked so hard to recruit. Boy, if she could take back that time she'd invested …

Saylor started toward her, looked at the AD, and then backed off.

Okay, maybe it wasn't so bad to have her boss in the gym.

They ran through the offense again and again and again. Then they ran it some more. She wanted them running it in their sleep. She wanted them telling their great-grandchildren how to run her motion offense.

When practice was over, her AD still sat in the folding chair. She approached. "So if something was wrong, you'd tell me?"

He stared at her for what felt like forever. "I want you focusing on your job. If this becomes a thing, I'll let you know. But for now, it is only a distraction." He gave her a tight smile, stood, and walked away, leaving her to wonder what on earth he'd meant by *becomes a thing*.

A thing? What thing? What kind of thing? And the thing that had everyone acting strange wasn't even a thing yet?

She felt worse than she had the night before. Maybe she needed to go get some more enchiladas. That thought brought Brad to mind, which made her miss him, and the missing surprised her.

He'd been a perfect gentleman on their date. She'd almost had fun. If there hadn't been a giant dark cloud swirling around her head, she would have had fun. But if there hadn't been a giant dark cloud, she would never have gone out with him in the first place.

She checked her phone. He hadn't called or texted. She was surprised. Maybe he'd decided he didn't like her as much as he thought he would.

That wouldn't be much of a shocker. Over the years, lots of people had decided that. She was too serious. Too driven. Too uptight. All the criticisms meant the same thing. She wanted to be good at life, she was willing to put the work in, and they weren't. So if they didn't like her, no big loss. If she wanted to fly with eagles, she couldn't be hanging around with turkeys.

Oddly, this made her think of Brad again. But no, he wasn't a turkey. She almost smiled at the thought. When he'd asked her out, she sort of thought he was. But he wasn't. Not really. So what was he?

Chapter 11

K yra's phone beeped as she got into her car to drive to work. A text from Brad: "Good luck tonight."

She sighed. She wasn't sure what to make of that. First, he'd waited nearly forty-eight hours to reach out to her after their date. Was he playing hard to get? If he didn't like her, he wouldn't have texted her at all, right?

She tossed her phone onto the passenger seat and started the car. It was too cold to sit there analyzing a text from a man she barely cared about. She had to get the engine warmed up.

She pushed her car to go faster than it wanted to, hoping that would encourage the hot air she needed blowing on her feet. She knew that real Mainers wore boots everywhere and then changed into "indoor shoes" when they got to where they were going, but she hated that extra step. So she was wearing dress shoes, and her toes were mad at her.

What had Brad meant exactly? *Good luck tonight.* He could have meant the game. That was a normal, casual, friendly thing to say to someone who was about to coach a college basketball game. But she wondered if he'd meant more than that. Maybe he'd meant good luck with the … the *thing* that wasn't really a *thing* yet.

She gasped. Did he know something? Had he learned something? Had he talked to Meghan? She pulled her car into the next plowed parking lot—it was a Gifford's ice cream stand, so why was it plowed at all?—and picked her phone up. She pulled her glove off with her teeth and wrote, "Thanks. For what?"

He answered immediately. Maybe he wasn't playing *that* hard to get. He sent a laughing emoji and then: "for the game."

Breath rushed out of her. Oh good. He didn't know anything. She was being silly. She dropped the phone and started to put her glove back on, but the phone beeped again: "And for everything."

Fantastic. *Everything*. What a loaded word that could be. She finished sliding her glove on and sighed again. *Stop being so paranoid*, she told herself and turned on her signal. So what if her girls were acting weird? Her athletic director, her *boss*, had told her there was nothing to worry about.

She pulled out into traffic.

But he hadn't said that, had he? Not exactly.

She tried to think about the game. She hoped Saylor would cooperate tonight. If not, she would have to bench her, and that would hurt them. She was fairly confident that they could win with Saylor on the bench, but it wasn't a given. Very little was in the world of Division III basketball.

Still, she would bench her if she had to. She couldn't let the girl walk all over her, especially since Saylor was only a freshman—a freshman who might well get herself cut during sophomore tryouts. Or maybe, during this year's exit interview, Kyra would suggest that Fort George wasn't a good fit for Saylor. Maybe she should find a better fit. Kyra's spirit lifted at this thought. She had two strong freshmen coming in next year. She didn't need Saylor.

Kyra pulled into the mostly empty field house parking lot and turned her engine off. Her car still hadn't warmed up, and her toes were freezing. She grabbed her bags and hurried inside, almost slipping and falling on her keister on the edge of the parking lot.

She opened the front door and relished both the warm air that rushed out at her and the quiet. The gym was such a peaceful place before games.

That peace wouldn't last long, though. She wiped her shoes off on the welcome mats and headed for her office. She didn't have much left to do, but she still liked to go through the motions of preparing.

Her office was blessedly warm, and she slipped her shoes off to give her toes a fighting chance at recovery. Then she went over the girls' matchups one more time.

Her mind drifted to Brad, and she reeled it back. Then a few minutes later, it drifted again. She almost laughed at herself. She had to get a grip. Did she really have a crush on the computer teacher? No, she did not. So if he was going to be this big of a distraction, she had to find someone else, someone worthy, someone realistic to have a crush on. She scanned her brain, flipping through the men she knew like a visual Rolodex, but she didn't see anything of interest, and then she was back on Brad.

Oh for heaven's sake. She stood up quickly and looked at the clock. She was still a little early, but she would head down to the locker room anyway. She obviously needed some external motivation to focus.

She put her shoes back on and stepped out of her office. The gym wasn't so quiet anymore. She strode confidently down the carpeted hallway, her brain ping-ponging between Brad and the game, and then she stepped out into the gym and ran into a wall of reporters and cameras. She startled but immediately recovered and put on her best professional public relations smile. Why were they here? They'd never shown up for a game bef—

"Ms. Carter"—a woman shoved a microphone into her face—"are the allegations true?"

Her blood ran cold as a cacophony of ravenous voices attacked her with varying versions of the same question. Her whole body tight with panic, she glanced over the crowd toward the bleachers where Brad usually sat, but he wasn't there yet.

There were only a dozen people in the stands, all of their eyes on her. Wildly she looked around the gym for her boss, but she didn't see him either. She tried to force a smile as the questions grew louder and more brazen—more demanding. It was as if they could feel her slipping away.

"No comment," she said, her voice sounding as if it had been dragged over gravel. She tried to push her way through them, but they tightened up to block her path. "Excuse me!" she said more loudly and tried to make her way forward.

"Don't you want to defend yourself?" a voice inches from her shoulder asked.

Kyra felt the first symptoms of a panic attack and pushed harder. She made it a few feet, but then the reporters closed in around her. Her body continued deeper into the panic as her brain tried to keep control. She wanted to plow through them. She was strong enough to do it. But she was in some sort of trouble, wasn't she? She didn't want to also be accused of assaulting reporters? And why were there so many of them? What could she possibly have been accused of to warrant so much attention?

"No comment," she said again and kept pushing. She was inching toward the door—but they were inching along with her. "Excuse me!" she said loudly, trying to sound strong and not frantic. She kept pushing. "No comment. No comment. No—"

"Enough!" a man's voice barked out somewhere in front of her.

The mob around her thinned a little as many of them turned to face it.

"Coach Carter has a job to do, and if you let her get to it, I will give you a statement!"

Most of them turned to him then, a few of them with obvious reluctance. Her boss's face came into view, and his expression read indignation, which was comforting, but she also saw some fear there. He nodded toward the door, obviously wanting her to flee, but she didn't want to flee. Not anymore. Now she was far more desperate to hear this statement he was about to deliver.

She made it to the door but then paused to turn and listen, holding her breath.

A warm hand slid into hers, and she looked up to see Brad had come alongside her. His coat was still cold from the outside air. He didn't look at her—his eyes were fixed on the mob—but body language suggested stalwart support, which nearly made her tear up. She turned to watch the show, trying to take deep breaths.

She'd only had about a dozen panic attacks in her life. This really wasn't a good time to meet number thirteen.

"Kyra Carter is an upstanding professional," Dave said, and she exhaled slowly. "These are baseless rumors circulated by disgruntled students. *Young* adults who will be held accountable for their slander and—"

A woman interrupted him with a question Kyra couldn't quite make out.

He didn't answer immediately. That couldn't be good. What had she asked? Kyra started to ask Brad, but then Dave spoke up. "Until someone comes forward with a specific complaint, I cannot take these rumors as anything more than—"

"Someone has come forward—" a man tried to interrupt, but Dave spoke over him, God love him.

"No one has come forward with a complaint."

"Yes, they have," the reporter said loudly, triumphantly, as if he'd won some contest, as if he hadn't just delivered Kyra's whole life a death blow.

Chapter 12

Kyra made it down a flight of stairs before the tears came. She backed herself into a corner and then bent and put her hands on her knees, fighting to control her breathing.

Brad put a hand on her back, and footsteps came down the stairs. She stood up and quickly swatted at her tears with the backs of both hands. She pressed into the wall, and Brad's hand felt so warm, so steady, like an anchor holding her there in place, keeping the panic from stealing her away.

Breath rushed out of her. It was only Dave. "I got some security at the top of the stairs," he said quickly. "You're good down here, I think." He ran a hand through his thinning hair. "But we've got to figure out a way to get you to your car."

"My car?" she said weakly. "What about the game?"

He gave her a bewildered look. "The game? Are you serious?"

Yes, she was serious. She didn't know how to be anything *but* serious. "Can't we just kick them out and play the game?"

She couldn't read his face. He stared at her.

Nervously, she looked at Brad, who was also staring at her.

He pressed his fingers into her back and looked at Dave. "She knows less than nothing about what's going on."

What? What did that mean? Did he know more than she did?

"Can you give her some more information?" Brad said.

Dave's eyes dropped to the floor, and he put his hands on his hips. "I don't know much …"

"Not much is a lot more than what she knows right now." Wow, Brad sounded almost aggressive. If not, then at least protective.

Dave lifted his eyes to meet hers. "I'm sorry that I didn't know. Apparently, one of your players told the campus counselor that she was having a relationship with you."

Kyra tried to make the words make sense, but they floated around in her mind in a jumble. "A what?"

Dave nodded slowly. "A relationship. Romantic, sexual, whatever, it's not good."

Her head fell back into the wall. This was going to destroy her. Just like that, her career was over. All that work. All those wins. All that sweat. All that time. All that pain. Nothing. Poof. It was all gone. Rode out of her fate on the back of one slimy, evil lie.

Dave reached out and laid a hand on her arm. "Obviously, it's not true." He didn't sound as confident as she wanted him to. "And I'll try to find out more ASAP. But for now, we need to get you out of the limelight. I'll coach the game."

"You?" she cried, sounding more appalled than she should have.

A small smile flickered across his lips.

"You're a football coach!"

"I know, I know. It's not ideal, but we just need to get through this night. Then I'll get to work trying to make this go away."

But it wasn't going to go away. She knew that. Her life was over.

"Go home. Have some wine. I'll call you in the morning."

Wine? Had he even ever met her? She didn't drink wine! "Morning? You expect me to wait till morning?"

Brad applied gentle pressure to her back. "Come on. I'll get you out to my car. We'll come back for yours later."

Her feet obeyed him before her mind had decided to. She told her feet to stop. "Wait." She turned back to Dave. "Let me talk to the girls."

His eyes widened. "That's not a good idea."

"Well, will you tell them what's going on? I don't want them to think I've abandoned them."

He hesitated. "Kyra, they all know what's going on." He glanced at Brad. "I think they've known for days."

The looks. The snickers. Of course they had known.

Brad tried to get her moving again, but, annoyed, she yanked her body away from him. "You think this is some sort of plan? They hatched it to get rid of me?"

Dave held out his hands, palms up, and shrugged. The gesture infuriated her. "I have no idea. I heard something a few days ago, so this didn't start tonight. But apparently, whoever it is, she only talked to the counselor a few hours ago."

Her brain spun. "Isn't it illegal for the counselor to repeat something like that?"

Dave furrowed his brow. "Not if the girl was asking for help, no." Oh no, now he sounded suspicious.

"Dave, I didn't do this," she said, stepping closer to him.

Brad started tugging again. "He knows that," he said softly.

This was absurd. How could Brad know what Dave did or didn't know? He didn't know Dave. He was just a high school computer teacher. "It was Saylor," she said matter-of-factly. She knew it with every cell of her body.

Dave slowly shook his head. "It wasn't Saylor."

"What? How do you know that if you don't know who it is?"

He exhaled loudly. He was getting frustrated. Frustrated with her? How was that fair? "I know it's a local girl."

"How do you know that?"

He held up both hands. "Go home, Kyra. Let me figure this out. I'll call you in the morning." He was angry now, though whether that anger was directed at her, she didn't know.

She turned and let herself be led away by Brad, who didn't speak until they were safely in his car.

She burst into tears.

Chapter 13

*W*hat am I supposed to say? Brad asked himself. There was nothing *to* say. Nothing helpful, anyway. But he couldn't just sit there quietly. That made him look like an unfeeling dufus. "I want you to know that I care, but I don't know what to say, so I'm not saying anything."

A weird half-giggle broke through her sobs. It sounded almost like a hiccup. "Thanks," she managed.

He'd never seen so many tears in his life, and he worked in a high school. "Do you want to go home? Or you could come to my place? Or I could hang out at yours?" *Oh man, am I making a mess.* "I mean, I'm not trying to invite myself into your home or anything, and I'm not hitting on you." *This mess is growing deeper and deeper.* "I mean, it's not that you're not worthy of being hit on, but I'm just not that type of guy." He laughed awkwardly and then tightened his grip on the wheel. *So, so deep.* "Or we could go get some food or a drink—"

Her head snapped up. "A drink? Why is everyone trying to get me to drink?" Her words shot out like poison darts.

"Whoa, whoa, I didn't mean alcohol. I meant like a Dairy Queen slushy."

She stared at him for a long time, long enough that he was able to glance at the road and back three times. She was looking at him as if she couldn't believe what she was looking at. Finally, she said, "Dairy Queen? It's twenty below out." And if he didn't know any better, it seemed she was almost amused. Still crying, still panicking, but now also amused. Was that even possible?

"You're right. Sorry. I don't think Dairy Queen is even open." He focused on the white and yellow lines in front of him, half of which were obscured by ice and snow.

But an odd squeak made him look at her again. Her shoulders were shaking. Oh wow, she was actually laughing. Still crying, but laughing too. He sighed. Good. That had to be healthy.

"Why does a slushy sound so good right now?" she said, her voice an octave higher than usual. She leaned forward and laughed harder as he frantically tried to think of a way to score her a slushy.

"I have no idea," he said slowly. It certainly didn't sound good to him. And apparently to no one else in the state because there was no place serving slushies this time of year—wait. "Would a gas station slushy suffice?"

She laughed even harder, edging the grief and terror the rest of the way away. Her whole body shook with laughter, and when she looked at him, her eyes danced. "Yes, I think so." She sniffed. "If they have cherry."

Oh my salt, he was going to spend the rest of the evening driving around the state looking for a gas station cherry slushy, wasn't he? "Your wish is my command." He pulled into the first gas station he came to and put the car in park. Then he looked at her. "Not really, in case your next wish is that I find you a pink unicorn."

She tipped her head back and laughed again. "A pink one? You had to specify a pink one?" She gasped for air. "So you could find me a plain old unicorn, as long as I don't ask for a pink one?"

Bewildered, he got out of the car. That afternoon, Meghan had given him a heads up about what was going on, but never in a million years did he think his evening was going to turn out like this.

It didn't take long to ascertain that there were no cherry slushies to be had at this particular Irving. There were two slushy machines, and both stood still and empty. He returned to the car.

Kyra was still smiling. "Aw, bummer."

"Never fear." He put his arm on the back of her seat, his hand brushing against her hair, as he turned to look out his rear window. He relished the feel of that curl on his skin as he backed up. Then he regrettably moved his hand back to his shifter. "That is not the only Irving in town."

She snorted and then took a deep breath. It seemed the laughter fit was over. But so too was the crying. "I don't think I've ever had a gas station slushy."

"Oh dear."

She looked at him. "What?"

"It is sure to disappoint."

She cackled, and he feared he'd set her off again, but this was just a quick, run-of-the-mill cackle. He stopped and waited for a break in traffic.

"Mmmm, Cumberland Farms. They have the best coffee."

The break appeared, and he gave it some gas. "Cumbies? I figured you for a Starbucks type."

She fake-gasped. "Who, me? I'm not a snob!" Her voice dropped an octave. "And I can't afford Starbucks."

He laughed and got out of the car.

There were no slushies at the Hartport Cumberland Farms in January. He returned to the car.

She had sobered. She looked at him through teary eyes. "Sorry that I sort of lost it there."

"No prob." He snapped his seatbelt into place. "It was definitely warranted."

She let out a long breath and looked out the window. "Yep, probably. But I still don't like to lose control of my emotions."

He didn't think she liked losing control of anything, but he didn't comment.

"Thanks for making me laugh," she said without looking at him.

"You're welcome." He pulled out of the parking lot, and they drove in silence for a minute.

"How many gas stations are there in Hartport?"

He did some quick counting. "Six, I think?"

"Wow. It's a regular metropolis."

Her deadpan delivery made him laugh again. This was so bizarre. They were in the middle of a crisis, yet he was having fun. That couldn't be right. But dang if it didn't feel good to have a mission.

"You don't have to keep trying." Oh no, was that sadness creeping into her voice?

"I'm going to get you that slushy if it kills me. If we can't find one in Hartport, there is always Wiscasset. And then Bath. And eventually, Portland. There *has* to be a slushy in Portland."

"I hear Piercehaven has slushies. Maybe we should take the ferry?"

This didn't make any sense, and he looked at her quickly to see one eyebrow quirked playfully. "Pretty sure the ferries don't run at night."

"We could steal one. Why not, I'm already going to prison."

Her joke hit their small space like a flood of ice water. He didn't know how to respond.

"Just kidding," she tried, but there was no levity in her voice.

"You're not going to prison, no matter what."

"I know." But she didn't sound comforted.

"No one is saying you assaulted anyone or did anything illegal."

"I know," she said, looking out the window. "Sure feels like that, though."

He pulled into the next gas station.

When he started to get out of the car, she put a hand on his coat. "Really, I was just kidding. Sorry that it wasn't funny. Funny's really not my thing."

Brad was overcome with an urge to lean across the car, grab her face with both hands, and kiss her till dawn.

Instead, he avoided her eyes. "I like your sense of humor." He got out of the car before he said more, before he said too much. He liked a lot more than her sense of humor, which was actually quite pathetic. Pathetic and somehow, perfect.

Chapter 14

B rad came out of the second Wiscasset gas station holding a giant slushy above his head like a trophy. Kyra couldn't believe how hard he'd worked for such a stupid, simple thing. What a sweet man. She was so touched that she almost teared up—but she didn't. Maybe she had cried herself dry.

He opened the car door and handed the frosty cup in to her before sliding in himself.

She didn't know what to say. Thank you didn't seem like enough, but she said it anyway.

"You, my lady …" He put his hand across his stomach and bowed forward into his steering wheel—"are very much welcome."

She giggled. "I can't believe you managed it." She looked around at the dark parking lot. "Who would have thought Wiscasset would be the place that all my dreams come true." She'd been kidding again, but talking about her dreams, even in jest, made her choke up. She tried to hide her emotions by taking a drink.

Flavor exploded in her mouth. What a sugar bomb this was. She hadn't had one of these things in more than a decade. Had they gotten more sugary, or had she just gotten old? She smacked her lips. "Delicious."

Wait. He was staring at her lips. How weird was that?

He realized she'd caught him and quickly turned front, busying himself with his ignition. "So, where to, now, my lady, now that our mission is complete?"

Where to? Where was there to go? It was too weird to go to his house or his apartment or wherever he lived, and she didn't want to go back to hers. "Maybe we could go get my car?"

He looked at the clock on the dashboard. "Already? I bet the game is still going."

"I know, but I doubt there are any people in the parking lot. They'll all be in the gym, won't they?" This gave her a thought. "Hey, do you know anyone there? Maybe you could text them, ask them the score?"

He looked hesitant.

Of course. He didn't want people to know that he was with her. That made sense. "Or not. Sorry. Never mind." She took another long pull through her straw and then took a break before she got an ice cream headache.

He looked at her. "You really want to go back to your car?" He sounded disappointed.

Not really, but what else was she supposed to do? "Sure."

"Okay then." He put his car in reverse and turned to look out the rear window. The lights from the gas station lit his eyes up and made them shine.

He caught her looking as he turned front and gave her a broad smile. She was glad there wasn't much light in the car because she feared she might be blushing.

What was going on with her? She really couldn't be crushing on this guy! Even if he was her only friend in the world. Wait, that wasn't true. He wasn't her only friend.

And even though her father wasn't her friend, exactly, she thought of him then, and her stomach rolled. He wasn't going to find out about this, was he? She couldn't let that happen. But what if she got fired? Could she hide that from him? Maybe, but it would be hard. She wasn't a good liar. And if she got fired in the middle of a season, she would have to move. And it would be hard to find work. How would she do all that financially? Especially without asking her father for help?

"I think I'm going to sue," she said, mostly to herself.

He didn't respond at first. Then, "I don't think we're anywhere near there yet. Let's see what your boss can work out. If some adults tell these girls the consequences of pursuing such lies, they'll probably back down and say the whole thing was a prank."

"Would they, though?"

He glanced at her. "Would they what, call it a prank?"

"No, would they face consequences? I can't imagine that anything will happen to them." She waved her hand toward the icy road in front of them. "They'll get to go on their merry way, get on with their lives, live long and happy, and I'll be stuck with the baggage forever." Her throat tightened again. She tried to take deep breaths to calm herself. She didn't need to sob any more in front of this man.

Or any more at all for this stupid situation at this stupid school in this stupid small town in stupid Maine. Why had she even come here? She'd been offered a job in Georgia at the same time. But that had only been a high school job, so she'd taken this one. "You know, I haven't been alone with very many of them." The realization gave her hope.

"Oh yeah?"

"Yeah. A few of them in my office, which I will never do again now that this has happened ..." *If* this wasn't the end of her coaching career. "But most of them, no. So maybe whoever my accuser is, if I've never been alone with her, then that could save me."

"Maybe." His lack of excitement annoyed her, and they rode in silence for several minutes.

"People are going to think I'm a lesbian."

He looked at her, the dash lights reflecting in his eyes.

"Like forever, for the rest of my life, there will always be this association."

"There are worse things," he said softly.

"I know, but ..."

"But what?"

"But I'm supposed to be a Christian." She wasn't sure how to put words to her fears.

Somehow, he understood them anyway. "Hey, your church will understand."

She wasn't so sure.

His dashboard dinged, and he chuckled. "So this is ironic, since we've visited seven gas stations this evening, but I need some go-go juice." He looked at her. "Do you mind?"

Did she mind? If the alternative was that they ran out of gas in the middle of nowhere and had to freeze to death walking to Hartport then, no, she didn't mind. "Sure."

"Cool. Thanks." They drove another few miles before a gas station came into view.

"Huh. That looks familiar."

He didn't laugh.

Figures. He'd been trying to be nice when he'd said he liked her sense of humor. Because she didn't have one.

He signaled and pulled into the parking lot for the second time that evening.

It occurred to her to offer him money. She winced. She didn't have any. She unbuckled. "Here, let me fill you up." She could use her credit card.

"No, no," he said quickly, nearly leaping out of the car.

"Please?" She leaned across the car to look up at him through his open door. "You didn't ask to drive me all over the state avoiding the paparazzi."

He laughed.

Defensive, she snapped, "What's so funny?" She knew they weren't really the paparazzi, and she knew she wasn't really a celebrity. Obviously.

"Oh nothing. I just like the way you pronounced that word. Made it sound extra Italian." He winked at her. "It was cute."

She sat up straight and looked straight ahead. He'd just winked at her? He'd just winked at her! Had she ever been winked at before? She didn't think so. She hadn't realized what a powerful effect a wink could have.

His voice drifted into her from closer to the pump. "Great. Now I'm craving pizza."

She waited for him to get back into the car before saying, "Pizza sounds really good right now."

"Yeah?" His excitement was adorable.

"Yeah. But I don't want to go in and sit somewhere if that's okay."

"Sure. You want some gas station pizza?"

She laughed. "No thanks. I think we can get all fancy and hit the first Little Caesars we see."

He joined her laughter. "Little Ceasars and cherry slushy. Do I know how to wine and dine or what?"

Food hadn't even occurred to her, but now that she knew pizza was coming, she was famished. She knew her hunger was at least ninety percent emotional, but she didn't care. If hot cheese would make her feel better, she would take whatever help she could get and deal with the consequences later. "But you have to let me buy this time."

Chapter 15

Kyra stood in the small lobby that smelled overwhelmingly of garlic. "Be about five minutes," the woman behind the counter said.

"Okay, thank you."

The woman's eyes lingered on hers for so long that Kyra worried she'd recognized her. Maybe she was a celebrity after all. Then she realized the woman was probably only wondering why she had black makeup smeared all over the upper half of her face. She turned on her cell camera and flipped it to selfie mode to confirm, and sure enough, she looked like a grounder from *The 100*.

Great. She turned and leaned against the counter and texted Brad. "It's not hot. Or ready. Five minutes."

It wasn't five dollars anymore either—when had that happened?—but she didn't tell him that part because she didn't want him to think she was complaining about paying.

"Do you want something to drink?" she sent.

"Sure."

She waited for him to be more specific.

He was not.

She started to ask and then decided it would be more entertaining to pick him out the strangest drink they offered. Her eyes scanned the offerings, looking for something offbeat—diet Fresca or canned Clamato—but saw nothing of the sort.

She wished she was closer to home so she could pick him up a Green River—now that stuff was refreshing, but alas, this godforsaken job had her pressed up against the Atlantic with only Coke, Sierra Mist, Orange Crush, root beer—and oh, wait.

There it was in black and orange: Maine's official state soda.

Moxie.

It tasted like root beer poured over mothballs. She'd been in Maine for two years and had yet to meet anyone who didn't hate it. She had no idea why Coke hadn't ditched the product years ago.

She would buy one for Brad, he would be mortified, but would also still probably be polite enough to force it down, and then she would laugh and tell him that he didn't have to do that.

She grabbed a non-moth-balled root beer as well to give him after the prank was over.

She paid for her beverages and pizza and headed back to Brad's car.

"How did we do?"

She bit back her smile as she handed him the orange-labeled bottle.

"Oh, awesome. How did you know?"

How did she know what? Was he messing with her?

He unscrewed the cap and took a long drink. Then he let out a long, satisfied sigh.

"It's you," she said in wonder.

"Huh? What's me?"

"You're the reason Coke keeps making Moxie."

He laughed. "Oh it's not just me. It's the whole state."

She shook her head. That had not been her experience.

He eyed the unopened root beer in her lap. "You could have had a Moxie and you got a root beer?"

She was confounded. "I'm from Ohio." This didn't make any sense, but those were the words that came out of her mouth.

He laughed as if she *had* made sense. "Still, you're an honorary Mainer now, and don't you know that Moxie is a tonic?"

Her confoundedness grew.

"Really." He took another drink. "It heals what ails you."

This reminded her of what was currently ailing her, and the distraction of the drinks and the funny man beside her dissolved away like fog clearing. Now she could once again see the giant screaming mess of a problem all around her, and she felt sick. She handed him the pizza and stuck the root beer in a cup-holder. "The root beer is for you. In case you didn't like Moxie."

"Are you okay?" He sounded sobered. Maybe the fog had cleared for him too.

"Not sure."

He didn't say anything for a minute. Then, "Want a piece of pizza?"

"Maybe in a minute. You go ahead." She knew the food would make her feel better, but she couldn't quite imagine the effort of chewing right now. "What am I going to do, Brad?"

"Right now, you're not going to worry about it. You're going to trust your boss, trust God, and trust that the truth will win." He took a bite of pizza and then added through a mouthful of cheese. "It always does, eventually."

She didn't know if this was true. She knew of a lot of lies that had won a lot of contests lately.

His phone buzzed, and he wrestled it out of his pocket, looked at it, and then quickly shoved it out of sight.

"What?"

"Nothing." He took another bite of pizza.

"Please tell me."

He gave her a long look. Was he evaluating her? If so, she would probably fail.

"Please. I need to know."

He took a breath and wiped his mouth on a napkin. "It was Meghan. They lost, and you now have two accusers."

Someone nearby made a weird barking sound. It sounded brittle. She wondered how a bark could sound brittle. Then she realized the bark had come out of her. She wasn't sure what to do with that realization.

"It's a good thing, I think." A floppy half-eaten piece of pizza cooled in his hand. He'd lost interest.

"How could that possibly be a good thing!"

"First, the school just found out that the team can't win without you. And them accusing you of having a relationship with two of your players is exponentially more absurd than one relationship. No one is going to believe that."

She wasn't as confident of that as he was. Coaches more successful than her had been caught in more complex scandals. Of course, those coaches had been men, but still.

Not for the first time, she wished God had made her a dude.

"Really, Kyra. Do you think people are going to believe you have a *harem*?"

The word made her chuckle, but the laughter didn't help this time. Her neck was so tight that her head hurt. "The game's over. I should be able to get back to my car now."

"Okay." He sounded sad. He set the floppy pizza on the dashboard and put the car in drive. "We can make that happen."

Chapter 16

Kyra got the text at six a.m. on the dot, as if Dave had been sitting there watching the clock waiting for an acceptable time to text. Not that six was acceptable, but she was very much awake. With the exception of a few fitful naps, she'd been up all night.

"Can you come in to my office early? Let's talk before anyone else gets there."

"Of course. What time?"

"As soon as you're able."

What, was he already there? She hurried to get ready and stepped out into the icy air at quarter to seven. She hurried to her car and then made the cold drive across town. The streets weren't exactly empty—there were already pickups going to and fro, but the streets weren't nearly as busy as they were during her normal commute time.

It was nice to be on the road this early. Maybe she'd start doing it regularly. She liked mornings.

That was, if she even had a job to drive to after today.

"Come on in, have a seat." He was trying to sound jocular, she knew, but his voice was strained. He looked tired.

She sat, careful to maintain good posture. She didn't want to look defeated. She wasn't. Not yet.

He folded his hands on the desk in front of him. "You know how highly I think of you."

No, not really.

"I was thrilled to hire you, and you've done a great job for us."

Here it comes, she thought, and she knew in that moment that she was going to sue the pants off this school. Her indignation had officially overridden her fear. She was done playing.

"I'm going to do everything in my power to make this go away."

Or maybe not.

"But it's going to take some time. Your accusers are not exactly willing to talk to me, and I've got to get some help, hire someone who knows how to navigate these situations. I don't want to muddy the waters mucking around trying to be a hero."

He leaned closer and lowered his voice. "So I will make it clear to anyone who will listen that this is not a punishment."

What wasn't a punishment?

"This is a suspension—with pay—pending an investigation, which I'm confident will clear your name, and then we can all get on with the season."

Well, not *all*. When she figured out who had done this to her, their basketball careers would be over. Maybe more than their basketball careers if she could manage it.

"Who are my accusers?" her mouth asked before her brain could stop it.

He slowly inhaled and then slowly exhaled. "Charlotte and Avery. But you didn't hear that from me."

That didn't make sense. Those two girls were quiet, hardworking, good students. Why would they want to stir the pot like this? She gasped. *Oh.* "Playing time," she said aloud.

He raised an eyebrow. "Beg your pardon?"

"The locals—some of them are mad that they aren't getting enough playing time." This was absurd, of course. Before she'd become the coach, the team only had locals, and they were terrible. She'd needed to recruit from away just to get them a winning season. And now these girls were punishing her for that? They would rather be losers than winners? They were insane.

"I don't know their motivations, not yet, but that's the least of my worries. I just need them to admit that they're lying. But until then, you get a mini-vacation."

Vacation? Hardly.

"Look, remember that I'm on your side, and right now it seems like I'm one of the few people who is—"

"Then don't suspend me. Please. Let me do my job. What happened to innocent until proven guilty?"

He gave her a patronizing look. "I know you're young, but believe me when I say that rule does not apply when there are kids involved."

These girls weren't kids. They were old enough to drink, smoke, sleep around, and tell ruinous lies—didn't that exclude them from the protection warranted a child? But she didn't say any of that.

"I'm sorry that I don't have more of a plan yet. But like I said, try not to panic. I've got your back, and I'm going to work on this." He leaned back in his chair. "And even if I can't fix it, worst case scenario is that I send you to your next school with a letter and a phone call declaring my belief in your innocence." His eyes rested on her in a way that suggested he was expecting gratitude now, but she had none to give.

She stood. "Can you please keep me posted?"

He nodded slowly. "I will."

She waited until she got back to the car before texting Brad. "Dave was cool, but I'm suspended. He says he's still trying to fix it." She wanted to say more, but it was only a text message.

He didn't answer immediately, so she added, "Have you heard anything else from Meghan?"

She was about to give up and drive away when her phone beeped. "I'm sorry. I'm praying. Nothing from Meghan, but I'll check in with her and you after school."

"Okay, thanks," she typed and tossed her phone on the seat. She leaned her head back. What was she going to do now? She was looking at one long, cold day.

No. Never mind that. He might not have time to check in with Meghan now, but she had nothing but time.

She mentally flipped through her roster. If she was going to start investigating, was Meghan the best choice? Kyra was intentional about not getting close to her players. Friendliness made discipline harder, so she always maintained good boundaries. But yes, there were a few girls she knew a bit better than Meghan. Meghan was always quiet, always just sort of there in the background.

But could Kyra trust Vicki or Daphne? Who knew how many of them were in on this scam? This wasn't merely some attention-seeking pot-stirring. This was an attempted coup.

Idiots.

What, did they plan to coach themselves? How many games would they lose before regretting that decision?

Or maybe not. Maybe they didn't care one iota about winning games.

She wouldn't contact any of them, then. She couldn't trust anybody.

She stepped into her warm house and felt relief. She kicked off her boots and crossed the carpet to sink into her couch. Then she looked around her home. What was she going to do now? The place was spotless. She was caught up on laundry.

She had nothing to do.

She looked at her bookcase, but she knew she wouldn't be able to focus on reading anything right now.

She picked up her phone, opened her Facebook app, and looked for Charlotte's profile. She couldn't find it. That was odd. Surely she had one? She looked for Avery's and couldn't find one for her either. She felt sick. Had they actually blocked her on Facebook? What on earth? She found Meghan's profile and then looked at Meghan's friends. Charlotte and Avery didn't show up there either, but that didn't mean anything. If they had blocked her, they wouldn't show up anywhere, right?

Saylor's name caught her eye. She clicked on Saylor's profile pic, which was of a basketball. And the very first post she saw stole her breath away.

Fort George Women's Basketball Coach KYRA CARTER is DISGUSTING. She has seduced multiple FEMALE players in a gross SEX scandal. Please support your local athletes by demanding that she be FIRED!

I'm going to lose my mind. The shame was overwhelming. She had to move. She had to do something. She threw the phone and stood. Her eyes fell on her sneakers. Perfect. She would go for a run. That would make her feel better. Even though it was insane to go running outside right now—slippery roads, salty slush, icy wind, and drivers looking at their phones—but she was going to do it anyway.

She put on the warmest clothes she could find and then laced up her sneakers.

Running was always a good choice. Pushing herself always made her feel better. Cardio would clear her mind, and she would be in a much better frame of mind after a quick five-mile loop.

Her legs started burning right away. Her muscles were too tight. Everything was too tight. Her lack of sleep were weights around her ankles.

Cold air stabbed at her burning lungs but did nothing to cool them. She ran and ran, telling herself it would make her feel better, waiting for it to make her feel better, wishing she'd brought her headphones so she could at least listen to some tunes.

She reached the road she needed to take to complete the five-mile loop, and she passed it. Five miles wasn't going to cut it today, and though she hadn't run more than a few miles since early fall, she was going to push it. She needed this. She needed to forget. Forget Saylor's gross Facebook post. Forget everything.

As she passed the Starbucks, two women in the parking lot turned and stared at her. She could feel their judgment zapping her like radio waves.

No, that was impossible.

How much could local people know already? It's not like she coached the Celtics.

Then she remembered the reporters and the cameras. Maybe they'd seen the news. Or maybe they'd seen Saylor's post. Now desperate for four walls and curtains on the windows, she took the next road that pointed her toward home. Maybe she should invest in a treadmill.

Seemed a little silly when there was one in the field house where she worked, but yes, she would get a treadmill for her living room.

Her cold toes and fingertips agreed that this was a fine idea.

Normally she would slow down as she neared the end of her run, a sort of unofficial cool down period, but today she could feel a million eyes on her back, and she picked up speed, running as fast as she could back to her house, up the steps, and inside.

She stretched out on the floor in front of her door, kicked her sneakers off, and cried a little. No sobbing. Only small, warm tears trickling out of the corners of her eyes.

Chapter 17

When Sunday morning rolled around, Kyra was thrilled with the prospect of going to church. She'd been holed up in her house since her icy morning run and was itching to get outside.

Brad had invited her out the night before, but she'd panicked and said no. She didn't know why she'd panicked, and by the time she'd realized that yes, she did want to go out with him again, it was way too late to change her mind without looking like a nut.

She was so excited to go to church that she considered going to Sunday school, but since she'd never been, she decided not to. It would be awkward to walk in and wander around looking for the adult class. Or the women's class. Or the singles' class. Or whatever class they would pigeonhole her into. Maybe they had a falsely-accused-college-basketball-coach class. She chuckled as she returned to her couch to wait out the forty-five-minute Sunday school period.

She picked up her phone to play Block Puzzle—there was something so mind-numbingly satisfying about turning all those little blocks into neat lines—and it beeped in her hand. She opened the message from Brad: "Want to go to church with me today? Would love for you to meet my friend Cindy. She's good in a crisis. It's sort of her thing."

Cindy? Her test tightened with an emotion she couldn't quite identify. Who was Cindy? Couldn't be too good of a friend if Brad had never mentioned her before. She started to type, "Who is Cindy?" but then thought that sounded needy or pushy or something else equally unpleasant.

"No thanks. Going to my church."

"Oh. Okay. Have fun."

She knew that Brad didn't have a high opinion of her church. He'd barely tried to hide that. And he had a point. Yes, they were the dress up and be quiet types, but that wasn't necessarily a bad thing. Life was a serious affair. She didn't want to go to a church that treated life like one big pizza party.

She made it to seven thousand in Block Puzzle and then lost. Well, that was frustrating. But it was almost time to go. She stood.

She couldn't stand to wait any longer. She had to get out of the house. She grabbed her purse and her Bible and headed for the door. She would drive slowly. Better to take her time getting there than to sit here for another five minutes.

This turned into spending five minutes in the church parking lot instead. She could go in early, of course, but getting there before the service started led to awkward conversations. She wasn't into those on a good day, and this was not a good day.

She didn't know if anyone in her congregation had heard about her recent woes. They probably hadn't since she hadn't heard from any of them.

This was a good thing. It would be like any other Sunday.

At 10:28, she headed for the door.

One of the elders blocked her entrance with his significant torso, and the hairs on the back of her neck stood up. He stepped outside, making her step back to avoid contact, and pulled the door shut behind him. "I'm sorry," he said, not even trying to sound sorry, "but it's not a good idea for you to worship with us today."

She was too dumbfounded to speak, and she knew her cheeks probably showed the heat she was feeling. In that moment, she hated her cheeks almost as much as she hated the man standing in front of her.

She didn't even know his name, yet he had this much power over her? She tried to stand tall.

"I'm sure you can understand. Our leadership has to consider all the factors and all the people involved. We have a testimony to uphold."

"I'm innocent," she said, trying to sound strong and sounding anything but.

He nodded, but his eyes were void of understanding. "When you're ready to rejoin us, call the pastor, and we can arrange a meeting." He turned to go back inside.

She was too shocked to move.

He turned to look at her as the door fell shut. "You should go." It wasn't a suggestion. It was a command. She'd just been bossed around by a power-tripping idiot in a thirty-year-old suit. She ground her teeth together so hard it hurt.

She turned and went back to her car. Furious. Ashamed. Cold. And tired. But most of all, disappointed. She'd really been looking forward to going to church today.

She texted Brad, "You were right. Should've gone to your church." She dropped the phone, not expecting an answer. He was in church like she should be. He wouldn't be checking his messages.

Her phone beeped.

Or maybe Greater Life people played with their phones during church services. "Come on over. I'll meet you in the parking lot."

Relief washed over her at the thought of seeing him. Suddenly, he was the most comforting thing she could imagine. But did she want to go to a new church today? Did she have that in her?

She stared at her phone. It was a little too late to back out now, and besides, now she could find out who this mysterious Cindy was.

She made the short drive to Pine Street and had to park on the road. Between the many cars and the sky-high snowbanks, there was no room in the parking lot. Better this way, she told herself, if she had to make a quick getaway.

She got out of the car and sighed. She was going to a pizza party. Was she overdressed? Brad hurried toward her wearing a slightly dorky sweater and ripped jeans.

Ripped jeans? To church? Her only friend was a heathen. She didn't really believe this, of course, but the thought made her smile.

"Welcome," he said, looping his arm through hers.

She appreciated that he didn't ask her what had happened at her church.

Maybe he didn't need to. He'd lived in this town a while. Maybe he had a pretty good idea of what had happened over on Gretel Street. Maybe that's why he'd invited her to go to his church in the first place.

He led her into a busy foyer and then into a busier sanctuary. The service had started, so why there were still so many people milling about, she didn't know. Brad seemed to know where he was going and led her toward the front with purpose. It occurred to her that he was going to drop her at the altar and leave her there, and she panicked a little, but he did no such thing. He brought her to a small opening in the front row, where he hollered over the music to introduce her to Cindy, who shook her hand with what felt like an unreasonable amount of delight.

Kyra tried to hide how silly she felt.

Cindy was old enough to be Brad's mother.

When the handshake finally ended, Kyra faced the front and tried to participate in the music, which was a bit rowdier than what she was used to. Still she managed to catch on—a little.

Brad's voice was adorable. He was off key, but she loved how much he didn't care. She sneaked a peek at his profile.

Oh my goodness, I actually like this guy. What is going on? Is it because I'm in full-on crisis mode, and any lifeline will do? Maybe, but she didn't think so.

In the end, the church service didn't much resemble a pizza party. Sure, some parishioners were a bit more ... relaxed than she thought appropriate, but there seemed to be lots of people in their Sunday best sitting up straight too. She appreciated the variety.

The music was good, and the pastor was smart, but she was still excited to get out of there. She'd squirted some gas into her God tank, and now she was ready to go home.

"Come over to my house for lunch!" Cindy said, her eyes smiling with a thousand lumens each.

No, most certainly, Kyra did not want to go have lunch at some strange, unreasonably happy woman's house. And yet there was a certain magnetism to Cindy. Her joy was contagious, comforting. Kyra didn't know her from a hole in the wall and yet around her, she felt ... loved.

Safe even.

It was super weird.

Cindy took her stunned silence as acquiescence. "Great! I've got to give a friend a ride home, but you two can go on ahead."

You two, she'd said as if they were a unit, a couple, a thing.

"Brad knows the way." Cindy started to walk away and then turned back. "Any food allergies or anything?"

"Yes, sorry," Kyra said. "I'm a vegan with a gluten allergy." She said it with a straight face, trying to be funny, but Cindy didn't even blink. She waved a hand. "Oh, good thing I stocked up on salad fixings, then!"

"Uh, she's kidding," Brad said.

Cindy laughed. "Oh, you silly goose! I'll see you there, then, and we'll grill some steaks!"

Kyra gave Brad a bewildered look. "Grill some steaks? Is she serious?"

He shrugged. "Not sure."

She must have been joking.

Nobody fires up the grill when it's ten below outside.

Chapter 18

B rad was pretty happy with Cindy. He would have to find a way to thank her later. She'd made it clear that she wasn't sold on Kyra as a potential partner for Brad, and yet she'd invited them over for lunch anyway. Either she was trying to help him spend time with Kyra, or she wanted to get a better look at Kyra for herself.

Either way, Brad was happy. When Kyra had turned him down the day before, he'd thought maybe he'd been sunk, but now here she was acting like they were old friends.

He liked being her friend.

Even if she never saw it as more than that, he hoped they would be friends.

He hoped she didn't get fired and move away.

He walked her to her car, once again noting what a nice car it was. Small college coaches must make a lot of money. Or she was a trust fund kid. "Cindy lives out in the boonies. If you want to drive your car back to your house, I can drive you out to Cindy's?"

She hesitated, and he thought he could read her mind.

"I promise I won't let you get trapped there. Anytime you want to leave, just say the word."

"Okay, sure. Thanks." She climbed into the car.

"Nice wheels."

She looked surprised. "Not really. Pretty basic."

Basic, yes. But new and shiny as well. Compared to his old beater, it was a Cadillac. He tapped its roof. "I'll follow you." He hurried back to his car. He wasn't sure where she lived and didn't want to get lost. Sure, he could call her for an address, but every chance he gave her to change her mind was one she might take.

Frustrated with the poky post-church-happy-and-in-no-hurry traffic, he resisted the urge to lie on the horn.

Finally, he got himself out onto the road and was pleased to see her sitting right where he'd left her. When she saw his car, she signaled and pulled out into traffic.

He followed her closely, still admiring her car, and then transferring his admiration to her house when she pulled into its driveway.

A cute little bungalow with what looked like a fresh paint job. He started to get out of the car, but she was already hurrying his way. Apparently she wasn't going to change into something more comfortable. But this was okay. She looked super cute in her dress and boots, and he didn't mind the little bit of knees peeking, even if they were covered in tights. He did manage to get the door open for her in time. "Nice place. Do you rent?"

She had slid into the seat and now she scowled up at him as she reached for her door handle. "First my car and now my house? Are you a closet materialist?"

He laughed and shut the door. It was too cold for outdoor banter, so he waited till he was back behind the wheel. "No, it's just a nice house. I was hoping you'd bought it and planned to live in Hartport forever."

She smiled, but it looked insincere. "No, sorry. It's just a rental."

Not a cheap rental. He gave it one last look in the rearview as he drove away, suddenly self-conscious about his old car, though it had been a stalwart companion for more than five years.

It's none of my business how much money she makes, he thought. And it didn't really matter. He certainly wasn't interested in her for her money. He almost laughed out loud at the thought.

"What's so funny?"

"Oh, nothing. I'm just in a good mood."

She seemed irritated by this. "Have you heard anything useful from Meghan?"

"No, sorry."

"And she doesn't go to your church?"

"She's been a few times, but no, not really. So far, she's not really excited about God. At least not that I've seen." He shifted in his seat. "She's in a tough spot."

"Oh really? *She's* in a tough spot?"

He wanted to be careful with his words. "You can both be in tough spots at the same time. Her tough spot doesn't make yours any less tough."

"Sorry," she mumbled.

"Nothing to be sorry about. I know your situation is horrible. But she's in a weird predicament too. Should she side with the coach that everyone hates? Or should she keep her head down and try to survive socially? And I'm sorry, but no matter how much I've told her that you're innocent, she's not entirely convinced."

"Oh," she said softly. Sadly.

"Don't worry, Kyra. The truth will win."

They were quiet for a minute. Then Kyra said, "She seemed to believe me in the beginning, when all this started."

"Yep, I think that she did. But her teammates have been pretty convincing." He was making things worse. He tried to think of a positive spin. "Despite all that, I'm confident that if she learned something concrete, she would tell me." What was she supposed to learn, though? Didn't he and Kyra already know everything?

"Are you taking me out to the woods to scare me, or does she actually live way out here in the willywacks?"

He laughed. "I promise, she lives out here. We're almost there." A minute later, he pulled up her long driveway.

"It's pretty," she said contemplatively.

He didn't think so, not in January, but he wasn't going to argue.

Cindy was there, and sure enough, she had the grill going. She flashed them a big smile. "Going to take it a little bit to warm up. Come on inside. We'll have some pre-lunch snacks."

They followed Cindy inside, and her dog Bruno rubbed his head against Kyra's leg. Brad wasn't sure what to expect—Kyra didn't really seem like a dog person, but he'd pegged her wrong. She knelt beside the dog and scratched behind both his ears.

Cindy laughed. "Oh, Bruno. You're such a flirt. Come in, come in! Let me take your coats!"

They shrugged out of their coats, and Cindy whisked them away somewhere. Brad sat on one end of the couch, and Kyra perched nearby. She looked uncomfortable, and she kept her eyes on the dog.

Cindy returned momentarily without their coats, but then she left again, leaving them in silence. Brad was still trying to think of something to say when she came back, carrying a small tray of veggies with a glop of white dip in the middle.

It looked like mayonnaise, and he shuddered.

"Here are some gluten free carrot sticks," she said, and set them down on the table.

Kyra laughed politely. She still looked uncomfortable.

Cindy sat in a chair and faced them. "So, let's take a stab at the elephant in the room."

Oh no. There was an elephant? What elephant? A few theories sprang to mind, and then he started to worry *which* elephant she was going to stab.

"Tell me what's going on with this coaching scandal."

Oh phew. Only *that* one.

Kyra was obviously stunned, and Brad fumbled to come to her rescue. "There's not much to tell—"

"I know," Cindy interrupted, "but she must know more than I know."

"I doubt it—"

This time Kyra interrupted him. "What do you know?"

Brad snapped his mouth shut. Apparently this conversation was going to happen. He reached for a carrot, careful not to let it touch the dip.

Cindy's eyes widened. "I don't know anything!"

"Are you sure? You strike me as the small-town busybody who learns things through osmosis."

Woah. That was a little harsh. Brad wondered if he should defend Cindy from this flatlander's aggression, but she didn't seem offended.

"Your assessment is accurate, but the college isn't really part of our town, and so nothing has come through my membrane yet."

Kyra's face cracked into a small smile, and her eyes fell to her hands. "All that I know is that two of my players have publicly said that they're having a relationship with me." She paused. "Which isn't true."

"What are you planning to do about it?"

Kyra looked up quickly. "Do? There's nothing I can do! My boss has banished me from the campus. I'm hiding out in my house waiting for him to save the day."

"Are you praying?"

"Of course I'm praying," she said, but Brad inferred she wasn't praying much.

"Good. I'll join you. And you'll let me know if there's anything else I can do?"

Kyra nodded.

"Good." Cindy got up, crossed the rug, and patted Kyra's knee. "I'm going to go check the grill."

Kyra watched her leave and then looked at Brad and mouthed, "Who is this woman?"

Brad wasn't sure how to answer that. "She's ... she's just Cindy." He knew what that meant, but he didn't know how to translate it for Kyra.

Cindy was back in seconds. "Still ice cold." She tee-heed. They were going to be here for a while. Cindy sat back down. "So when is your next game?"

"Home game Tuesday against Machias."

"Oh! Are they good?"

Kyra hesitated. "We shouldn't be taking any teams for granted. Am I worried that we could lose to them? Yes, definitely."

"So what are you going to do about that?"

Kyra gave him another bewildered look. "As I said, there's nothing I can do."

"Oh bosh. Does anyone tape the games?"

"Yes," Kyra said slowly, "but they're not livestreamed or anything."

Cindy looked at him. "Can't you hack into that or something?"

Brad laughed. "Hack into what, an offline video camera? No, you overestimate my technology skills. And what good would that do? Then she could watch them lose? She still wouldn't be able to do anything about it."

Cindy gave him a dirty look. "Well, can *you* film it?"

"What?" He was both entertained and annoyed.

She spoke slowly, as if explaining it to a child, but she didn't sound confident in what she was explaining. "Can't you film it on your phone and put it on YouTube or Facebook or that clock app ... what is that called?"

"TikTok?"

She snapped her fingers and pointed at him. "That's the one!"

"Yeah, I don't think that's how TikTok works."

"But can't you put it on one of those websites so that she could watch it as it is happening?"

"Yes, but still, what good would that do?" Why was Cindy being so dense?

"I don't know," Kyra said thoughtfully.

Uh-oh.

"You could just FaceTime the game to me."

"Yes!" Cindy chirped. "What's FaceTime?"

No one answered her.

Cindy looked at Kyra. "Who is coaching your team?"

"My boss, the athletic director."

"Great. So put a tooth in his ear and talk to him while you're watching the game that Brad is showing you."

Kyra's eyes widened, and her head snapped toward Brad.

He still didn't understand. "Put a *tooth* in his ear?"

"She means Bluetooth," Kyra said quickly, "and I think that would work."

That was insane. "Would he do that?"

Kyra shrugged. "I don't know, but I doubt he wants to lose."

Brad thought maybe she was overestimating her coaching abilities. Was she really going to watch a game on one phone and then coach the game through a different phone? Would that really be any better than the job that Dave would do?

"Will you do it for me?" she asked, her eyes pleading.

Of course he would. He would do pretty much anything.

"Thank you, Cindy!" Kyra chirped. "You're a genius!"

Genius wasn't exactly the word he would have chosen.

January 17

Dear Frank,

I was wrong.

I know you'd tell me to say that again, so I will. I was wrong.

Wrong about the basketball coach.

And while I've been wrong before (and admitted it!), I can't believe I was so wrong about her. But I'd heard so many people talking about what a monster she was, about how she hated her students. I was told that when her player collapsed from a drug overdose, the other players rushed over to help, and she hollered at them not to, told them to keep practicing. I'm sorry, but that is a monster!

But that story doesn't at all match the lovely, meek woman I chatted with today. (I guess that's what I get for idle gossip—you know, till just recently, I always thought that was "idol gossip" because it was people sitting around talking about the private lives of movie stars, their "idols" haha!)

Anyway, she has this cute way of saying things with no expression. Deadpan. So I don't know if she's kidding. And then her jokes aren't very funny, so I'm always wondering if I should laugh.

But the way Brad looks at her erases all my doubts.

He is really in love, and if she loves Jesus AND makes Brad that happy, then she's a winner.

Okay, I'm starting to get drowsy, my love. Talk to you again soon.

Love,

Cindy

Chapter 19

B rad felt incredibly conspicuous holding his phone up in the air and
following the ball up and down the court. What grown man goes
alone to a women's basketball game and then films it on a puny phone?
There was no way anyone would assume he was on official business for
the college.

And he wasn't, not really.

And he'd been totally unprepared for the physical challenge of this
chore. He wasn't exactly in primo physical condition. Only two minutes
into the game, and his arms were screaming to be put back down on a
computer keyboard, where they belonged.

Kyra had ended up with two Bluetooth headsets—one for each ear,
one for each phone call—so she could simultaneously holler at him to
move the camera three degrees to the right and holler at her boss to tell
Daphne to force Machias' shooting guard left.

"What just happened?" Kyra demanded directly into his eardrum. He
wanted to turn down the call volume, but that would make the camera
wiggle, and then she'd holler at him some more. "What just happened?"
she said more loudly. As if it was her lack of volume that had made him
not answer the first time.

When they were alone together, just talking, he loved the sound of her voice. It was a soothing, lilting alto that sort of mesmerized him.

Now she sounded like one of his mother's hens panicking when the dog got too close.

"Will you please tell me what happened!"

He did not want to do that. He was surrounded by people. It was weird enough that he was videoing the game. He didn't need everyone to also know that he was on an active phone call, and worse, *who* he was on an active phone call *with*.

"Brad? Are you there?"

Oh my salt. He lowered the camera so he could text, "I don't really want to talk in the middle of the bleachers." He quickly snapped the camera up again, his arms protesting.

"Sorry." She said quickly and then was quiet for a minute. Then, back to her lovely alto, "Thank you. I really do appreciate this."

He was curious if she was giving Dave much feedback. Every few minutes, Brad would watch the AD, looking for clues that he was listening to someone in his ear, but this took Brad's attention away from his filming task, and Kyra would holler at him again.

"I don't mean to be critical," she said, and he could tell she was trying to sound patient, "but every time you sweep to the left, I can't see the corner closest to you."

Why would she need to see an empty corner of the floor?

The next trip down, he made sure to get that corner shot, and sure enough, a forward was camping out there. How had she known? Had she noticed that one of their players was missing from the screen?

Dave started hollering at someone to go cover that girl. So this was actually working. Unreal.

Brad wondered how long Kyra's suspension would last and how many more games they had this season. He didn't want to do this many more times.

But he also knew that for her, he would.

"Show me the clock," she barked for the tenth time, and he pointed his camera at it. He heard the first part of another word, but she got cut off. She must have switched to her other phone call.

Sure enough, Dave hurriedly told a girl to get into the game, but then as she ran by him toward the scorers' table, he grabbed her arm and pointed to a different girl. The first girl looked sad and sat down, but then a now frenzied Dave grabbed her again. Brad bit back a laugh. Apparently Kyra wanted *both* of those girls in the game. He wished he could hear her conversation with Dave. He was betting it was pretty entertaining.

"Iris!" Dave hollered out onto the floor.

Saylor stopped moving and stared at him blankly.

Who was Iris?

Dave closed his eyes for a few seconds, probably listening intently to his marching orders. Then his eyes popped open. "Fighting Iris!" he cried.

A crazy image flashed through Brad's mind: two bearded irises wielding two tiny swords at each other. What a blood bath.

Saylor was shaking her head. "Do you mean Irish?"

He didn't answer her. "Can you hear me?" Brad muttered.

"Yes," Kyra said quickly.

"Tell him it's Irish, like the leprechaun."

Kyra didn't answer Brad, but two seconds later Dave yelled out, "Leprechaun!"

Saylor looked annoyed, but one of the girls he'd recently put into the game figured it out and started yelling "Irish! Irish! Irish!" as she went to get the ball.

The girls spread out above the key, and Brad realized Kyra had been trying to get them to run a stall. He didn't know why she would bother when they were behind. Maybe she was trying to get the last shot? One of the girls from the bench set a screen—and held onto the shirt of the defender as she tried to fight by it.

Well, that wasn't exactly good sportsmanship. Had Kyra taught them that?

The girl she'd screened for dribbled into the paint. Her defender was pinned behind her, but she quickly drew three more as the pinned girl's teammates came to help.

The dribbler ran right into them, and the whistle blew. She flopped to the floor, her limbs all akimbo.

Brad glanced at the ref, half expecting a call of offensive foul—or unsportsmanlike chaos—but the ref had his hands on his hips. Interesting. There had definitely been contact, but he wasn't certain that Kyra's player had been fouled. She certainly hadn't been fouled hard enough to flop down onto the hardwood like a shot partridge.

Looking unscathed, she peeled herself off the paint for a one and one. She drained them both, sending Fort George into the locker room with a one-point lead.

Awash with gratitude, Brad turned off his camera, leapt up out of his seat, and weaved his way through the crowd, his arms singing praises as gravity brought blood and oxygen back to his fingertips. "Excuse me. Excuse me." He didn't push, but he moved with intention, counting on the sea to part. He only had a few minutes, and he wasn't content to wait for the slow shuffle.

As soon as he was outside, he said, "Are you there?"

Nope, she wasn't. He checked his phone to see if he was still connected, and he was, so apparently she was talking to the other guy.

Of course she was. She needed to eavesdrop on their halftime meeting.

Brad hung out near the smoking section, wiggling his fingers.

He was about to head back inside when Kyra jumped the tar out of him. "You there?"

He nearly yelped. "Yeah. How are you doing?"

"Not great. This is impossible." She said this as if the plan had been his idea. Then she seemed to feel bad about snapping. "How are you doing?"

It didn't seem very manly to complain about the pins and needles in his fingers. "Fine. Hey, did that girl just fake a foul?"

"No," she said tersely. "She *drew* a foul."

"Okay."

She hesitated. "She might have exaggerated a little."

"And that girl who set the screen? She held onto the girl's jersey—"

"Shh!"

He looked around. "Why are you shushing me? No one is listening to me."

"Well, I've got enough problems without you spreading rumors about me playing dirty."

"Rumors? Are you serious? A whole gymnasium full of people just watched the same play I did. You don't need me to spread rumors."

"Well, they don't notice those details when we're winning." She sounded defensive. And tired.

"So, it's win at all costs?" He winced. That had sounded judgier than he'd expected.

"Of course not. But it's win or nothing else matters. That's the way the world works."

"So that's what Irish is? Girl dribbles into the paint and falls down?" He knew he was being combative, but he couldn't seem to help himself. He was annoyed.

"Of course not. Irish means that Madison sets a screen, and Avery draws a foul."

"Why can't she just draw it from her own defender?"

"A lot easier to draw it from the help that's rushing toward you." Now she was treating him like an imbecile. "Would you please go back inside?"

Maybe not. He was tired of this. And hungry.

She sensed his annoyance. "Look, I'm sorry. I'm ... I'm a little stressed out right now. It's not easy coaching a college basketball game through two phones."

The world would not end if she didn't coach it.

Fine. He headed back inside. "So that's Avery's only skill? I don't think I've seen her play before."

"She's not very good, but her foul shot percentage is about ninety. That's why I taught her to draw the—" She didn't finish the sentence. "I think they're getting ready to start."

He had stepped back into the gym now and could clearly see they were not ready. She just hadn't wanted to admit that yes, she had been the one to teach Avery how to fall down in the paint. How off-putting. Maybe Brad wasn't as smitten with Kyra as he'd thought.

No one was beautiful enough to make up for cheating and manipulating.

He eyed the back row. Some spots had opened up. Whoever had been sitting there would likely return and be annoyed that he'd stolen their seat, but he stole it anyway. It felt good to lean back against the cold cement.

He got his phone ready and waited for the whistle.

Chapter 20

K yra felt a hundred percent like a stalker. She sat in the field house parking lot before the sun came up, waiting for her boss to pull in. She had no idea if he regularly got to work this early, but he'd gotten here this early at least once, so she had hope.

If the place filled up before he showed up, then her plan wouldn't work.

A truck she didn't recognize pulled into the lot, and she slid down in her seat, only her eyeballs and forehead sticking up over the wheel. If he saw her, he would assume she was a seven-year-old pretending to drive.

But he didn't see her. Or at least he pretended not to. Not for the first time, Kyra gratefully noted how good Mainers were at minding their own business. He drove by and kept going toward the maintenance buildings.

She exhaled slowly. This wasn't a big deal, she tried to reassure herself. It's not as if there was a restraining order against her. No one had told her that she couldn't be on campus.

But she still didn't want to get caught. She felt so needy, and she didn't like it.

But she had to talk to Dave.

And there he was.

Half expecting him to spot her or at least recognize her car, she waited for him to head her way, but he didn't. She watched him get out of his car, lock it with his fob, take ten steps, turn and lock it again, and then walk into the building.

She scanned her surroundings and then quickly followed him.

He didn't look surprised to see her slip into his office.

"Sorry." He sat and wheeled his chair toward his desk.

Oh no. "For what?"

He gave her a perplexed look. "For losing."

Oh yeah, of course. What else would he be sorry for? None of this was his fault, not even the losing.

She glanced at the chair. "May I sit?"

He sighed. "You really shouldn't be here."

"Are you telling me to go?"

He hesitated and then motioned to the chair. "I'm telling you that you don't have a lot of people on your side here, and I don't want you to run into someone who will be less than supportive."

"Why?"

"Why, what?"

"Why don't I have anyone on my side? People actually think I did this?"

He finally looked at her. "I don't know, Kyra. I'm not sure they've given it much thought. I think they don't like you, and now they have an excuse to express that."

A lump sprang into her throat, and she didn't dare try to talk around it.

He rested his elbows on his desk and rubbed his face with both hands. "Sorry, that was a little harsh."

A little?

He dropped his hands and looked at her. "The important thing is *I* am on your side, and I am trying to fix this."

His tone made it clear that it wasn't going well. "So losing last night's game is the least of my worries?"

He shook his head quickly. "I wouldn't say that. I appreciate that you still care about your team's performance. But I am wondering if the whole Bluetooth thing is worth the effort. I think I might do better on my own than trying to coach, communicate with you, and then do what you tell me to do."

She disagreed. "If we lose this next game, we are in serious trouble."

"That's not true. So what if you go into the tournament at a low seed? I'll make sure you're back in time for playoffs, and then you can clean up this mess. You can beat any team in this conference, so let's just let the chips fall for now, and then you can make up for it in the tournament."

That was a downright stupid gamble, but she wasn't going to argue with the only one on her side. This made her think of Brad. He was on her side too, right? And Cindy too. Quite The Dream Team.

"Please," she said. "Give me one more chance. I'll be less demanding this time."

He shook his head slowly. "Sorry. It's just too crazy. I'm not an idiot. I can coach a girls' team through one basketball game."

"I know you can. I didn't mean to say that you couldn't." She drew a shaky breath. "Do you think it would be helpful if I talked to them? Maybe I could try to get them to see reason." He tried to interrupt her with an argument, but she kept right on talking. "I could ask them why they're doing what they're doing, I could apologize, I could—"

"No! You should not have *any* contact with them until this is resolved."

"But—"

"Kyra, I know this is a terrible situation, but maybe you're overreacting."

She almost screamed in protest.

"It's not like there's a criminal aspect to this. They are both old enough to be considered adults by the law, and no one is saying you forced anyone to do anything."

Her stomach rolled. She bit her tongue hard enough to hurt. Did he think that's what she was worried about? Prison?

"As I've said before, the worst that can happen is I can't get you reinstated."

That wasn't the worst. The worst was that she wouldn't be able to find a better job, not with this hanging over her head.

His next question surprised her. "Why does Saylor hate you so much?"

"How do you know she hates me?"

He gave her a long look that suggested everyone on the East Coast knew that.

"I don't know. Saylor has a contrary personality—" And just like that, she realized why Saylor hated her. She gasped and looked at Dave. "There were rumors about Saylor having some sort of thing with Jennifer Lane."

"It was more than rumors."

She frowned. Why did the AD know more about her players' personal lives than she did? "So maybe Jennifer is still mad at me about booting her."

"I'm sure she is, but I doubt that's why Saylor is mad."

"Huh?"

"From what I understand, Jennifer dumped Saylor right after all that happened."

"Oh, even better." She felt sick. Saylor probably blamed her for the breakup.

"You had to remove her from the team, Kyra. She broke contract. She used a controlled substance—and a lot of it."

She nodded. She knew that. "I don't regret booting her. I just wish Saylor wasn't out to get me."

"I'm not sure she is. This has nothing to do with Saylor. This is Charlotte and Avery."

She knew he was wrong about this, but she couldn't explain how she knew that, so she said nothing. "Thanks for your time. It's getting late. I should go."

"Of course."

She felt his eyes on her as she headed for the door.

"Kyra?"

She paused, turning sideways. She didn't want to look at him. She didn't want him to see how defeated she was.

"I really am trying to fix it. Try to hang in there."

She nodded and left the room. She could hear people milling about the building now, so she kept her chin up as she left, but she didn't feel any of the confidence she was faking. *Father, fix this, please.*

It would take a miracle for her to survive this. Even if Dave did fix it, it wouldn't be over. She would always have this black mark on her reputation. She would need to move a zillion miles away. She would never trust another player again. Her life as she knew it was over. She stepped out into the frigid air, but she was still sweating as she got into her car.

All that hard work reduced to a shameful nothingness.

She started the car and tried not to spin her tires in her hurry to get off the campus. *Maybe I'll never come back here again*, she told herself. The idea brought momentary comfort, but she had no fantasy to replace it with.

If not this, then what? There was nothing else. All she'd ever done was basketball. All she'd ever wanted to be was basketball. Her junior year in college, when she'd finally faced the truth that she wasn't going to be good enough to go pro, she started laying the groundwork to be the best coach the world had ever seen.

And now this.

She'd done nothing wrong. *God, how could you let this happen to me?* Was he punishing her for something? She didn't see how. She worked really hard to live a sinless life. She didn't party or sleep around. She had a disciplined thought life. She was a good steward of her resources, including her physical health. *Then, why, God?*

She shook her head. This woe-is-me line of thinking wasn't going to do any good. She had to focus on winning the next game. *Just do the next thing, Kyra.*

Chapter 21

B rad held the phone with his left hand and lowered his right to allow blood to travel back to those fingertips. Then, when it had, he would switch and give his right hand a break. He wanted to kick himself for not investing in a tripod between the last game and this one.

He looked at Dave enviously. That man had been smart enough to get out of this ridiculousness. But oh no, not Brad. When she'd asked him to stream another game to her, he hadn't balked.

He thought he might balk next time.

Because Brad Foster was losing interest in Coach Kyra Carter.

He'd known she was focused—he'd even liked that about her. But this, this was beyond focused. This was obsessed. He was starting to think that there really wasn't anything else to this woman. Only basketball and this obsession with winning.

Part of him knew this couldn't be true. She was a follower of Jesus. God had created her. There had to be more to her.

But whatever this "more" was, she was keeping it so deeply buried that Brad no longer had the ambition to dig it out.

"Hello?" she said, and he realized he'd forgotten to follow the ball with the camera.

"Sorry," he said, and swung it left.

"No worries. Hey, I really do appreciate this." She was in a better mood now because her team had a ten-point lead.

He just wanted this game to be over. Meghan still wasn't getting any minutes, even with Dave coaching. Brad was bored.

He became less bored when Husson began to chip away at Fort George's lead.

Saylor was stinking up the floor. Her teammates weren't doing much better.

"He really needs to pull her out for a few minutes," Kyra said for the tenth time.

Brad didn't respond. He didn't want to talk to himself in this crowd, and she wouldn't listen to him anyway.

"Hey, scoot over to the other side of the gym and tell him to take Saylor out, would you?"

Fear struck him. Was she serious?

"Kidding."

He quietly faked a laugh.

Kyra was quiet for a few minutes, but when Husson sank a three-pointer to take the lead, she made a weird whining noise.

Brad listened closely for a clue as to what that noise had been. It had almost sounded like a wheeze. But no clues were heard.

He pressed his headset into his ear. "Kyra?" he whispered.

"Yeah."

Yeah? That was it? "You okay?"

"Yeah." She didn't sound okay. She was breathing hard, and her voice sounded strained.

"What's wrong?"

She sucked in some air. "I ... trouble ... catch ... my breath." More wheezing.

"I'll be right there." He jumped up and climbed out of the bleachers.

"No ... I'm okay ..." The weakness of her protest further worried him. Something was wrong. Was she having a heart attack? She was way too young, of course, but he knew stress could do crazy things to people.

He was at her house in five minutes.

He didn't hear anything, so he tried the door. It was unlocked. She looked up at him; she was pale and panting.

"Hey." He stepped inside. "I'm going to call the ambulance." He ended his call with her and dialed 911.

"No!" she cried with strength that encouraged him. Dying people couldn't be that loud. He clicked the red button to end the call before an operator answered. Then he went and sat beside her on the couch.

She held up a finger. "Just ... minute."

"Kyra, I really think you need medical attention."

She shook her head. "Just ... panic ... attack."

This was *not* a panic attack. Over the years, he'd seen dozens of his students having panic attacks. They did not look like this. This was something worse. Her entire body was fighting for air. "We don't need to call an ambulance. I could take you to the—"

"No!" she snapped.

He looked at the door. Could an ambulance transport someone against their will? He didn't think so. He discreetly texted his paramedic friend. Then he put a hand on her back. Hard to believe that only minutes ago he'd been trying to convince himself he'd lost interest in this woman. Now that she was in trouble, he knew how laughable that was.

She continued to struggle. It was an unbearable sound. He wished he knew how to help her. He wished he knew what was wrong with her so he could look up how to help her. "Is it asthma?"

She shook her head.

He checked his phone to see how long it had been since he'd texted Trace.

Three minutes.

Since he hadn't texted Superman, he still had a few minutes to wait. "Do you want some water?"

She shook her head and tipped over. This scared him for a second, until he realized she was only trying to lie down. He picked her legs up and laid them across his lap. "Hey, can you open your eyes please?" If she could, that was a good sign, right?

She did. "I'm ... okay," she said again.

"I'll believe that when you can breathe." Was this some kind of allergic reaction? Did she need an Epi pen? "Do you have any allergies?"

She closed her eyes again.

He considered throwing her over his shoulder and taking her to the hospital. He looked at the door, willing Trace to burst through it with answers.

Her breathing did not improve while they waited, and Brad stopped trying to figure out what was wrong with her. He silently prayed instead. That Trace would get there, that she would be okay, that it wasn't anything serious.

Kyra jumped when someone knocked on the door.

Chapter 22

"Come in!" Brad called. He could have gotten up and opened the door, but he didn't want to leave Kyra.

Trace came inside and knelt in front of the couch. "Hi there. My name is Trace, and I'm a paramedic. Don't try to talk if it's too hard." He looked at Brad. "Remind me of her name?"

"Kyra Carter.

"Hey, Kyra."

"She's the coach at Fort—"

"Yeah, I know. One gloved hand pushed her hair back off her face.

Absurdly, Brad reacted to this with some envy. Embarrassed, he silently repented for that.

Trace's other hand felt her wrist for her pulse. "Can you open your eyes for me?"

She did.

"Good job, Kyra. I'm going to ask you some questions, okay? But I don't want you to try to talk. I want you to concentrate on your breathing, okay?"

She nodded.

"Good, good. Okay, I want you to breathe in through your nose."

Panic flickered in her eyes.

"Do it with me. Ready?" Trace dramatically inhaled through his nose. Brad was surprised when Kyra mimicked him. Trace was good at this.

"Good, good. And then exhale through your mouth. Like this." He did it with her. "Good, good. Keep doing that, and we'll get you fixed right up. Now, squeeze my hand if the answer to any of these questions is yes. Ready?"

She nodded.

He smiled. "Nodding is a lot of work. Just squeeze my hand, okay?"

She nodded again, briefly smiled, and then squeezed his hand.

"Good job. Okay, Kyra, do you have any pain in your chest?"

Brad stared at their joined hands. She didn't squeeze.

"How about your head?"

Still nothing.

"Either arm?"

Nope.

"Either leg?"

Nothing.

"Do you have any pain anywhere?"

Nothing.

"Good, good, that's great news. How about tingling or numbness?"

She squeezed.

"That's okay. Nothing to worry about. In your hands?"

No.

"Feet?"

Yes.

"Anywhere else?"

No.

"Okay, that's good." Trace looked around the room. "Do you have any pets?"

No.

Trace looked disappointed.

"A pet?" Brad said. "What does that mean? Is this an allergy thing?"

Trace ignored him. "Kyra, I think you're having a panic attack."

She squeezed his hand hard, and Trace chuckled. "Have you had a panic attack before?"

She squeezed again.

"Okay. That's helpful in a way. You lived through the last one, so you know you'll live through this one, right?"

She didn't look convinced.

Brad felt like an idiot. He'd had no idea that panic attacks could be this severe. He really, really wanted to avoid ever having one of his own.

"Keep breathing. We're going to get you better, okay?" Trace looked at Brad. "Sometimes petting a furry friend helps ease the symptoms," he said quietly. "Wish I had my little guy with me. He would help for sure. Good job, Kyra. Keep breathing. That's good. Do you have any prescriptions for anxiety?"

She shook her head.

Her breathing was getting better. She was still struggling but not as much.

"That's okay. Do you want me to take you to the hospital?"

She shook her head quickly.

"Okay. I'm not going to make you do anything," he said quickly.

The two men watched her breathe, watched her recover. Eventually, she slowly sat up, and Brad was sorry to have her legs leave his lap.

She put her head in her hands. "I'm sorry. I didn't need you to come," she said slowly.

Brad expected Trace to be offended, but that didn't appear to be the case.

"May I recheck your pulse?"

She stuck her hand out.

He pressed his fingers to her wrist and concentrated. "Good," he said after several seconds. "That's much better." He let go of her and stood. "I can still take you to the hospital if you want, but I am also confident you're going to be okay."

"I know I'm going to be okay," she snapped.

Trace's feathers remained unruffled. For the first time, Brad wondered what sorts of verbal abuse his job subjected him to on a regular basis.

"Thank you," she said with more humility. "I didn't need you ..." She shot a look at Brad. "But I do appreciate you coming." She took another deep breath through her nose.

"You bet." He looked at Brad. "You all set here?"

Brad nodded. "Thanks, man. I owe you one."

"Good because I'm pretty sure Shelby got us a virus downloading pictures of Cavalier puppies."

Brad snickered. "You're getting a puppy?"

"That's what I hear." He headed for the door. "If you need anything else, don't hesitate to call." He looked at Kyra. "Feel better, Coach." Then he was gone.

Brad waited for her to speak, and she made him wait a long time.

Finally, she said, "Can you text Meghan, see if they lost?"

He couldn't believe it. He slid closer to her on the couch and boldly put his arm around her shoulders. He opened his mouth to challenge her, to say something along the lines of, "What on earth is wrong with you? It's just a stupid basketball game." But a gentle, quiet voice suggested he say no such thing. She was going through a lot. A few minutes ago, she hadn't been able to breathe. "I don't know if the game's over yet, but sure, I'll text her." He typed a quick message and hit send, hoping she wouldn't answer for a while. He had a bad feeling about her answer and wasn't sure Kyra was in any condition to receive it.

Meghan answered immediately.

"What'd she say?"

He didn't want to tell her.

She groaned. "Oh no." She put her head in her hands.

"Kyra, it's okay, it's not that big—"

"Okay?" She looked at him through wide, red eyes. "It's not okay!"

He sucked in some air. "No, I know. I mean, the situation stinks, but the loss isn't that big a deal."

She glared at him.

He didn't know what to say, so he didn't say anything.

"You know what ..." She was exhausted, but at least she was breathing normally now, almost. "Thanks for coming, but I'd like to get some rest."

Oh. He stood up quickly. "Okay, sorry. Didn't mean to overstay my welcome."

"No, no." She slowly got to her feet. "You didn't."

And then, just when he was thinking this really couldn't work—ever, at all—she took his hands into hers and looked deep into his eyes. "You can't imagine how much I appreciate you." She leaned in closer. "And though I wish you'd kept filming the game"—even her chuckle sounded tired— "I do appreciate you rushing over here to be my knight in shining armor." She kissed him on the cheek, leaving him so bewildered he did nothing to respond. Then she let go of him and stepped back. "Someday I'll try to make all of this up to you, but today is not that day." She forced a smile.

He wanted to take her in his arms and hold her tight. Then return her sweet, innocent kiss—but he didn't. "Okay." He grabbed his coat. "Call or text if you need anything."

"I will." She followed him to the door.

He turned back. "Are you sure you want to be alone? I mean, I get why you don't want me here." He chuckled awkwardly. "But maybe I could call Cindy? Just so someone would be here with you?"

"No. I'm okay. Really."

"Okay," he said reluctantly.

And then she closed the door behind him, and he had no idea how to feel. He was falling for her, but he was also worried that this was never going to work, which led him to think maybe he should try to stop falling for her.

Chapter 23

Despite everything, Kyra couldn't help smiling on her way to church. It wasn't that she was excited to be attending the pizza party church, and it wasn't that she was feeling healthy and well rested.

She was thinking about Brad. About how she hadn't been able to sleep the night before, and somehow, he had sensed it and had checked in on her at one in the morning.

"Why are you awake?" she'd answered him.

"Misery lights out my window."

She'd laughed aloud. "Misery lights?"

"You know, the flashing blues."

"Why are there flashing blues? Have they finally come to arrest you for underachieving?"

He'd paused before answering, and she'd worried she'd offended him. "Sorry, got distracted by the reality show outside. No, they're not here for me. My neighbors are fighting again."

"Oh. Bummer." She hadn't known what else to say.

"Want a play by play?"

"Sure." She had nothing else to do.

So he'd led her, step by step, through the sheriff's department conflict de-escalation process. That had taken them through till two, and though she knew she shouldn't laugh at others' troubles, a few of the moments were comical. One of the men involved tried to throw a stick at a police officer, but it was attached to the tree he was leaning on.

Eventually, Brad had sent, "I should let you try to sleep now."

And though she didn't want to stop texting with him, she'd said, "Okay. Good night."

But he didn't stop. Instead, he started sending her a steady stream of funny TikTok videos. It had started with a drunken man running into a tree branch, which at least had some connection to recent events. But the next videos he sent had no connection to anything. Highlights included: a break-dancing gramma; a dog refusing to get out of a swimming pool; and a teenage boy trying to dribble a snowball.

She'd never spent time on TikTok before. She'd always thought it was a waste of time, but these videos had her in stitches.

"I think the sun's going to come up soon," he'd typed. This was an exaggeration. They weren't perched atop Mount Cadillac, but she figured he must have been flagging.

"Right," she typed. "Get some beauty sleep. I'll see you at church."

"Awesome. Good night, beautiful."

Such a silly, simple little compliment, but she'd fallen asleep with a smile on her face, and that smile was still hanging on. She signaled to turn into the church parking lot, musing over the fact that though this was the most miserable, turbulent time of her whole life, she was still managing to squeeze some joy out of it, thanks to Brad.

Brad. She shook her head. She couldn't believe she had a crush on a computer teacher. Oh well. There was no use fighting it, and if he was a lawyer or an entrepreneur or anyone else she'd pictured herself dating, he probably wouldn't have been the type to sit with her through her insomnia. He would have been too worried about getting enough sleep to tackle his day ahead.

She didn't think Brad ever tackled days. More like he let them wash over him.

And there he was. Standing by the front steps with his hands in his jean pockets, waiting for her. How romantic.

She got out of her car, zipped up her coat, and headed his way.

He reached out and took her hand, and then gave her an unexpected kiss on the cheek. His lips were warm, and she was sorry when they left her skin. She smiled at him.

"Tired?" he asked, smiling back.

"Not bad."

"Great." He started up the steps. "I'd be some embarrassed if you started snoring during the sermon."

She followed him into the sanctuary. She didn't think she could fall asleep during this pastor's sermon. He hadn't been boring last time.

Cindy left her front row seat to come join them in their pew. "How are things?" She smiled brightly.

Kyra didn't want to answer that. She didn't want to think about it. "Pretty much the same."

Cindy nodded as if she already knew that. "You know, I have an idea."

Kyra waited for her to say more.

"I don't want to meddle, but—"

Brad snorted.

Cindy looked at him quizzically, waiting for an explanation for the snort, but he didn't offer one.

Still smiling, she continued. "I feel like we need some sort of catalyst, and I feel like God might be the best bet."

Kyra had no idea what she was talking about and looked to Brad for help, but he didn't offer any.

"Brad, can you ask Meghan to help?" Cindy said.

Brad looked annoyed. "What can Meghan do? She has nothing to do with any of this."

Kyra's good mood was rapidly dissipating.

"I think I know a way she can help."

Brad stared at Cindy. "I don't want to upset Kyra, but Meghan doesn't want to help. She wants to stay out of it."

Cindy's smile didn't fade, but she furrowed her brow. "Doesn't she know that Kyra is innocent?"

Brad's irritation was growing.

Kyra shifted uncomfortably in her seat. She didn't want to be stuck between these two while they argued.

Brad sighed and looked at Kyra.

She had a pretty good idea what he was thinking. "Go ahead, I can take it."

His eyes slid to Cindy. "I think on some level, yes, Meghan knows that. But either way, it's certainly unfashionable to side with the accused these days. The girls don't really like Kyra ... sorry ... and so Meghan's not going to risk her social welfare to stick up for her when she might be out of the picture soon. Then what will Meghan have gained?"

Cindy looked horrified. "But this is about what's right and wrong!"

"I know that!" Brad snapped. "But it's not that simple for Meghan. Can we please just leave her out of it?" The music started, nearly drowning out his last words. He stood, his body language dismissing Cindy's big idea before it was shared.

Kyra looked at Cindy, who sat staring up at Brad. Kyra put her hand on Cindy's. "Thanks for trying," she said loudly.

Cindy gave her a small smile, but it looked sad. She patted Kyra's hand and then stood up and started to sing.

Kyra stood too, but her good mood was completely gone. She didn't want to be in church at all now. She had told him to go ahead and speak the truth, but she hadn't expected the truth to be that harsh.

If he was right, she was sunk. No one was going to stick up for her. A lump formed in her throat. She didn't bother faking singing. She just stood there, leaning on the pew in front of her, waiting for church to be over.

As the first song gave way to the second, she thought about quitting. She didn't want her name attached to this season's record anyway. Maybe that was the answer. Maybe she should just ride off into the sunset like a good cowboy.

But that would mean leaving Brad. Her emotional brain told her this was a bad idea, but her rational brain quickly overruled. Yes, Brad was sweet and fun, and yes, she liked him. But there was no future in this. She certainly wasn't going to spend the rest of her life in Hartport, even if this did all turn out in her favor.

Hartport was only a step on the ladder to where she really needed to go—the top.

So then, she should quit. Give up. Stop throwing good money after bad. They didn't deserve her. She would hold her chin up and walk away.

The interminable music finally ended, and Kyra gratefully sat.

Cindy leaned over and whispered into her ear, "I'm not giving up."

Kyra appreciated the gesture, but it was moot. There was no point to Cindy fighting if Kyra was going to give up. She would tell her that after church.

Chapter 24

Brad could feel Kyra's discomfort. She had sat stiff as a board through the entire service. Maybe he shouldn't have said what he'd said. Maybe she didn't know how much her team disliked her.

The service ended, and Cindy smiled at them brightly. "Would you guys like to come over for lunch?"

Before he could answer, Kyra said, "No, thank you. I'm a little over-tired. I need to go home."

Cindy's smile fell. "Okay then." She reached out and patted Kyra's hand. "Just remember, you're not alone in this." Then she was gone and talking to someone else, probably about their problems.

Kyra looked at him. "I've decided to quit."

He felt his eyes go wide. "What? Why?"

Her mouth laughed, but her eyes didn't. "Why? Are you serious?"

He was suddenly very tired. Maybe he shouldn't have spent all night watching TikTok. "Yes, I'm serious. If you quit, it will make you look guilty."

"I look guilty no matter what. There is no way out of this. I'm lucky that Dave is on my side, but he's the only one."

Ouch. That smarted a little.

"Either I hang around till I'm fired or not rehired, or I quit. At least then it's on my terms."

But she couldn't just quit. Then she'd move away. They would be over. Not that there was really a *they* yet, but he'd thought they were on their way to a they.

Then suddenly, he knew the words that would change her mind. "Kyra. If you quit, they win."

Her jaw dropped. She didn't say anything, but he could tell that it had worked. She could never let anyone else win—at anything.

Instantly, he felt guilty. He'd manipulated her. "I know you're tired, but can we go get lunch somewhere and talk?"

She nodded. "House of Salsa?"

He laughed. "Sure. Come on. I'll drive." As he stood, he tried to take her hand, but she subtly dodged his grasp. It was so graceful, he could have assumed she hadn't meant to do it, but he knew that she had.

She stood too. "No, it's okay. I'll follow you. Then I can go straight home after. I'll really be ready for a nap after all that cheese."

Fair enough. They walked outside together and then went their separate ways. There was a cold wall between them now. Hard to believe how readily she'd accepted his kiss on her way in. How had he managed to mess up that badly in ninety minutes?

The short drive felt long, and he was relieved to see her car in the House of Salsa parking lot. Part of him had expected her to flee, to quit right then and drive to the next state on her career path.

But she hadn't fled, and he slid into the booth and faced her. "You look beautiful today."

"Thank you." His words had no effect on her. Terrific.

He waited till they'd ordered before saying anything of value. Then he took a deep breath. "What's the most important thing in the world to you, Kyra?"

She gave him a dirty look. "What?"

He didn't say anything. He knew she'd heard the question.

"God."

The correct answer. But not the one she really believed. Of course, he couldn't exactly call her a liar. Then she'd really be mad.

"What's the second most important thing?"

"I don't know," she snapped, "people, I guess? What are you doing, Brad? If I wanted to be quizzed, I'd watch *Jeopardy*."

He chuckled. "Good one."

Her eyes smiled a little, suggesting there might be a small crack in the ice wall, but her mouth was more disciplined.

"I'm not quizzing you. I'm trying to understand you."

"What's there to understand? I'm not complicated."

This was not true. "You, my dear, are very complicated."

She stared at him. "No. I'm the simplest person I know. You want to know why?" He'd never seen her so defensive. The exhaustion was making her vulnerable. "Because I know that the world is black and white. It's not gray like everyone tries to make it because they don't have the strength to face the truth. It's black and white, right and wrong, winning and losing, up and down. Life is not nearly as complicated as people try to pretend it is, and they pretend this because of their own weaknesses, because they don't have the courage to face the facts."

Whoa. His brain told him to run for the hills. This was so not the woman for him.

His heart, however, had other plans.

Chapter 25

Kyra's life was spinning out of control. She knew she was saying too much too fast, but the words just kept spilling out, rear-ending each other in their hurry to embarrass her. She snapped her jaw shut, but it popped open again. "I don't make excuses. I do what I need to do to make the most of this life, and I'm not going to apologize for that. If people don't like me because I do well at life, well then that's not my problem."

It felt like her problem, but she tried to convince herself that it wasn't. Her father had taught her, *If you wouldn't ask someone for advice, then you shouldn't care about their opinion.* Thinking of her father made her eyes hot, and she silently begged them not to betray her. *Don't cry. Don't cry. If you do, Brad is going to think you're crying over this stupid team and what he said in church. He won't know you're tearing up because you thought of your father.*

"So forgive me if questions like what's the second most important thing in life feel a little too much like naval gazing. I don't have time to sit around contemplating nebulous ideas. You know what's important? Cold hard results." She folded her arms across her chest and nodded for punctuation. There. Maybe now she'd be able to stop talking.

Brad studied her. Surely he would lose interest in her now. And that was okay.

It was a long time before he spoke. And when he finally did, his question caught her totally off guard. "Do you have any siblings?"

"Yes. A brother." She didn't want to talk about him.

"Older? Younger?"

"Younger." Where was he going with this?

"Does he have a name?"

She sighed. "Ezra."

He smiled. "Ezra. A Bible name."

"Yes. My father is a pastor."

His eyebrows flew up, and this annoyed her.

"Don't act like you just gained some insight into me. I told you, I'm simple."

"Why don't you have a Bible name?"

She hadn't had to answer this question in a long time, but she was still tired of answering it. "I do. I'm named after Cyrus. Female form is Cyra, but my mom wanted to use a K. They fought about it. She won."

His eyes widened. "That's so cool! *Cyrus*."

"He let the Jews go home from Babylon."

"I know who Cyrus is." Brad's eyes sparkled.

She shifted in her chair.

"And he didn't want to name you Rachel ... or Deborah?"

She wrinkled her nose. "He wanted a boy. He expected a boy. He wanted to name him Cyrus. He got me."

"And then Ezra. Wow, your dad is really into the rebuilding of the temple."

She couldn't help it. A small smile broke through.

"Surprised he didn't keep going, get a Nehemiah and a ... sorry, I can't think of anyone else."

Her smile fell, and she busied herself straightening her fork. "Me neither." She exhaled. "My mother died giving birth to Ezra."

He gasped, and she glared at him. "Again, stop analyzing me."

He reached out and grabbed her hand. "I'm so sorry, Kyra."

"It's okay." She thought about pulling away but decided against it. "I barely remember her. He remarried. I have a stepmom. It's not like I was an orphan." She didn't want to talk about this. How had she gotten herself into such a personal conversation?

"Are you close?"

"Me and my stepmother?"

"Your whole family."

She shrugged. "I guess."

"So family is important to you?"

She glared at him and pulled her hand away. "What is your point?"

He looked sad. "Just that family is important to most people."

"Yes, Brad, I love my family. I'm not a sociopath."

The food arrived, just in time, and Brad leaned back in his chair. As soon as the server left, Brad said, "Okay, it's obvious you don't want to talk to me, so I'll drop it and let you enjoy your lunch. But since you asked, my point is this: I think you focus too much on winning."

She bristled, but he didn't give her a chance to argue.

"The truth is, no matter what you do in life, you've already won anything that matters because of the victory of the cross. All you're doing is running around in circles trying to win meaningless contests, which, frankly, I think is a waste of time. And yes, I'm wondering why you're like this. Forgive me for wanting to know you. I guess I can stop that soon, when you leave town to go find a new meaningless contest to win. But yes, while I had you here, I was trying to figure it out. Why you are like this. Why being successful is so important to you." He picked his fork up, and she opened her mouth to argue, but he kept going. "Because you know what? Most people who are driven to be successful? They chase success because they think it will make them happy. But that doesn't appear to be the case for you. You don't appear to want to be happy—"

"Life isn't about my happiness," she snapped. She couldn't take it anymore. She'd grown up in a preacher's house. She didn't need a sermon from her boyfriend. The thought made her cheeks hot, and she looked down. This man was not her boyfriend. At least, not anymore.

"Obviously. And I didn't say it was. Life is supposed to be about Jesus, and what is Jesus? He's patience, peace, compassion, grace, forgiveness, mercy, kindness ..." The longer his Jesus-list went on, the angrier he got. "You know what? Never mind! I'm not feeling or acting very Jesus-like myself right now, so I'll stop. I'm sorry, Kyra. I care about you. *I* want you to be happy. I want you to enjoy life. I want you to have peace." He looked down at his plate and pushed his food around with his fork.

"It's not that I don't have peace," she said quietly. "It's not fair of you to judge me based on what you've seen the past few weeks. This is a stressful time."

He looked up at her. "You're joking. I watched you all last season. I watched you in the beginning of this season. I've never seen peace."

"Well, no one is peaceful during a basketball game! That's the whole point! It's supposed to be exciting!"

He started shaking his head before she finished her sentence, which annoyed her. "That's not true. There are peaceful coaches. Loving coaches. Happy coaches."

She didn't know how to argue that. "Good for them."

He dropped his fork and slid his chair back. "Maybe we should ask for some to go boxes. I really do want you to enjoy your meal, and I don't think that's going to happen if we remain in each other's company."

Something in her chest twisted painfully. She didn't want him to leave. "I'm sorry. I didn't mean to ..." She didn't know how to finish that sentence.

"I know you didn't. And I'm not mad at you. I think we're just too different. We have different worldviews."

"No," she said softly. "I don't think we do."

His eyes softened. "No?"

She put her fork down too and focused on him. "We agree on all the big things. We both know what matters. You're just ... laid back. Type B personality." She forced a smile. "I'm an A."

He chuckled. "Try triple A."

Oddly, she was a little flattered by this.

"Does winning make you happy?"

The question surprised her, and so did her answer. No. It didn't. Not really. But she wasn't about to admit that.

She didn't have to. He could read her mind.

"Then what does?"

Nothing. Nothing made her happy. "I guess I figure I'll be happy when I get to the end of my life and know I've done my very best."

He smiled. "That's a good goal."

Whoa, it was? She'd expected him to argue.

"I'm sure you're familiar with what happened with Mary and Martha, right?"

It took her a second to realize he was back to the Bible. He'd said their names like they were personal friends of his, like he was about to tell a story that happened a few days ago.

"Yes, I'm familiar, and yes, I know that I'm a Martha."

He furrowed his brow. "Do you ever try being Mary?"

She started to get annoyed again, and she didn't want to be annoyed with him. "Nope." She tried to sound playful.

He wasn't having it. "But you know that Jesus said that Mary chose better than Martha?"

"I also know that God said to be holy in all I do."

Brad smiled. "Ah, and we're back to the Old Testament."

She didn't answer that. She looked around for a server. It was time to ask for some boxes.

"But holy doesn't mean perfect."

Her eyes found his.

"You try to be perfect, don't you, Kyra? The perfect hair and make-up"—he glanced up at her hair—"the new car, the nice house, the best clothes—"

"I didn't say that I try to be perfect. I try to be *holy*. I'm not stupid. I know that none of that has to do with real holiness, but we are judged for everything, and I do want to make God proud." She took a quick breath. "Not *perfect. Holy*. Because I'm told to be." She wanted to look away but the light in his eyes held hers there.

He cupped his hands and held them out to her like he was offering her an invisible gift. "God said, 'Be holy like me.' I don't think it was a command. I think it was a gift. What if he was saying, 'Here, here is my holiness. My gift.'"

A shiver ran up her spine.

"And gifts aren't earned." He dropped his hands. "They're *gifts*. They're free. Free to you because of Jesus." He leaned closer, and she could see love in his eyes. Was that love for her or for his subject matter? Or both? "Kyra, the only holiness you'll ever obtain is that which God has gifted you through Jesus. You can't be holy on your own, no matter how hard you work."

Tears sprang to her eyes, and she looked down. "If I wanted therapy, I'd pay for it."

He laughed. "I don't want to be your therapist. I want to be your friend." He took a big breath. "I'll leave you alone as promised. But Kyra, I've really enjoyed getting to know you these past few weeks. In fact, I'm crazy about you. And so I want what's best for you. I want God's will for you. And I don't think God's will is for you to run yourself ragged trying to be perfect."

She took a long shaky breath. If she talked, she'd cry more.

Brad waved to a server and politely requested boxes. The server looked at their plates, obviously confused.

"Something's come up. We have to go," Brad explained.

"I've never loved anything the way I love basketball," she admitted. She was no longer feeling defensive, exactly, but she wanted him to understand. She wasn't as bad off as he was making her out to be.

He nodded, listening intently.

"I was built to be a basketball coach. I know that's what God wants from me. And a coach who doesn't win isn't much use."

He smiled and took her hand again. "I have no doubt you will be the best coach this world has ever seen, Kyra Carter. But you can do that while being loving, patient, and kind. You can do that while being at peace in your life, in your heart."

The boxes arrived, and he let go of her hand to fill his. She took the other box and with shaking hands, scraped her food off her plate.

Then it was time to go. She forced a smile. "You're a good man, Brad Foster. I'm glad I got to know you too." Then she left, trying not to cry anymore.

Chapter 26

Kyra ate her Mexican food without tasting it. Then she took a short, fitful nap.

Immediately after waking, she got up and started to pack. She didn't want to contact Dave on a Sunday afternoon. She would talk to him in the morning. Give him a letter of resignation and ask him for a letter of recommendation.

In the meantime, she could get ready to go.

As she packed, Brad's words ran through her mind. She could hear his voice like he was right there. She could remember his exact words.

A lot of them had been right.

And some of them had been wrong, though the more she thought about those wrong words, the less wrong they seemed. She was *not* a perfectionist. She wasn't stupid. She knew that only Jesus was perfect. But she did strive to be like him. To be the best. To be sinless. To be clean and new and sharp.

Was all of that vain? She didn't think so. But a new idea had dawned in her head. What if she already was sinless, clean, new, and sharp—not because of what she'd accomplished in her life, but because of what Jesus had done on the cross?

That's not the way she'd been raised, that was for sure.

It wasn't that her father had taught her that she had to earn Jesus' love. It hadn't been like that. But there had been this constant pressure to earn Jesus' approval, hadn't there?

Her phone rang. Foolishly, she hoped it was Brad, but she didn't recognize the number.

"Hi, it's Cindy!"

Oh boy. "Hi, Cindy."

"Hey, really quick. I'm still working out the details, but I just need a firm commitment from you that you'll be at Greater Life next Sunday."

Huh? "Uh ... I don't know."

"Not good enough, sweetie. I need you to say yes. I've got an idea, but I need you there."

She had planned to be back in Ohio by Sunday. "What's your plan?"

"It's going to work."

That's not what she'd asked. "What does that mean? What are you planning to do exactly?"

"It's going to clear your name."

She snorted. Yeah, right. Little late for that.

"I'm serious."

Her hands stopped packing, and she hesitated. "What do I need to do?"

"You need to pray all week and then show up on Sunday."

"That's it?"

"That's enough. Praying all week isn't easy."

She chuckled. "Is Brad part of this?"

"No, and don't tell him. I don't think he's going to be happy with me."

Conspiring against Brad gave her a silly thrill. "Okay," she said before she was ready to commit.

"Great. See you then. Gotta run." She hung up.

Kyra slid her phone into her pocket and stared at the half-packed suitcase. She moved it onto the floor, leaving it open with her clothes in it. No use in unpacking.

But now what?

Probably no use in writing a resignation letter yet either. Not for another week, at least.

She sat on the edge of her bed. Apparently it was time to start praying. She knelt beside her bed. She hadn't knelt to pray in years, but it seemed now was a good time to start again.

"God," she said aloud and then felt foolish and continued the prayer in her head, *I don't know what to say. I don't know what to ask for. Cindy told me to pray, but I don't know what I want.*

She paused to gather her thoughts.

I guess I could ask for some wisdom. About this situation for sure. Do I quit? Do I fight? Do I even want this job? But also for everything that Brad said. I know about Mary and Martha, God, but I'm really, really good at being a Martha. If we're all Marys, wouldn't Christians all be sitting around doing nothing all the time?

It occurred to her that Cindy had just ordered her to be a Mary for a whole week. Oh boy. This might kill her. She smiled.

I thought I understood who you are. I thought I understood who I am in you. But Brad confused me. Have I got some of this wrong? Don't you want me to work hard, to be like the ant? Don't you want me to do my best, to be a winner, to give you a good reputation? Oh, wait. I guess your reputation doesn't really need my help, huh? She laughed quietly. *Yeah, so I'm definitely asking for wisdom. Please tell me what you want. Please.*

Chapter 27

I t had been the longest week of Kyra's life.

And against all odds, it had also been the most peaceful.

She hadn't prayed right straight for seven days, of course, but she had prayed as much as possible. And she'd read the Bible a lot. The Bible that, for the first time in her life, seemed to contradict itself:

Don't sin—You have been set free from sin.

Be doers of the law—You are not under law.

Faith without works is dead—Salvation is not a result of works.

Always do your best—Relax and be like Mary.

Work hard like the ants—Cease striving.

Her head was spinning.

So she was excited to go to church. She would finally find out what Cindy had up her sleeve, and she also hoped she'd glean some wisdom from the service. She hoped the spinning would slow down.

She got into her car a half hour early. She couldn't stand to wait anymore.

The first thing she saw when she stepped through the doors was Madison's face. Her young eyes grew huge on eye contact with her coach.

Oh no. What had Cindy done? Kyra scanned the room, looking for other players, but her eyes found Brad instead, and she immediately relaxed. She hadn't talked to him at all in the preceding week, but she saw nothing in his expression or body language to suggest he was upset with her. Instead, he waved her over.

On her way to his pew, she saw another player—Ella. Yep. Cindy had done something stupid.

Only when Kyra stepped closer to hug Brad did she see Meghan sitting beside him. Meghan avoided eye contact, but Kyra still didn't think it was appropriate to not greet her, not when she was two feet away. "Good morning, Meghan," she said and sat down on the other side of Brad. She didn't expect a response, and she didn't get one, but that was okay.

Brad sat too and took her hand. This surprised her. They'd basically had a fight a week ago and hadn't interacted since. Why did he think he could take her hand? But she didn't rip it away, so maybe he knew something she didn't know.

Did he know something she didn't know?

She leaned to him and whispered, careful not to let Meghan hear her, "What did Cindy do?"

He subtly shook his head. "I don't know yet," he mumbled back. Then he squeezed her hand. It occurred to her that he'd only taken her hand to demonstrate to Meghan that he had Kyra's back. Not exactly romantic, then, but it still made her tummy warm.

After a week of doing mostly nothing except chatting with God, she still didn't know whose worldview was right—her work-as-hard-as-possible-and-win-as-much-as-possible worldview or his kick-back-relax-and-hang-out-with-God worldview.

He let go of her hand when they stood to sing, and though this was disappointing, she thought it might be for the best. She didn't want to get too attached. She didn't want to miss him when she left.

After the music and several redundant announcements, the pastor went to the front of the room without stepping up onto the platform. "I love it when you guys have great ideas. Please don't ever think that the leaders of your church are the only ones who have big ideas because we're not. I was so excited when Cindy brought this idea to me, and I jumped on it right away."

Kyra held her breath.

"Many of us know that here in Maine, the sport of basketball is a god, especially in winter, especially to our kids and their families. Our church, and I know others like it, lose a lot of attendance to games and practices. But instead of complaining about it and judging those families who have to make those tough choices, and trust me that those are tough choices, Cindy thought we should reach out and connect with these families. What if we tried to participate in their lives? What if we tried to connect with them outside of these walls? So that's what we're going to do. Cindy drew up a schedule." He pointed at the screen behind him, where a list of schools appeared. "Each week, we've invited a local team to join us on Sunday morning. We will honor them during our service, honor their commitment to their sport and their hard work, and we will pray for them. Then, as many of us as possible will commit to attend one or more of their events that week, and beyond if you want to."

A disgruntled murmur rippled through the back of the room.

Darren chuckled. "This is all voluntary of course. I know a loud gymnasium and hard bleachers aren't for everyone. But I hope some of us will participate. I can tell you that a family who misses church all winter feels pretty awkward coming back in the spring. So many of them just don't. I can also tell you that some sports families feel judged by some of us. So what if, instead of judging them, we went to their kid's game and loved that kid? Supported that kid? Showed that kid that we still care about him or her, that they are still a part of this family of God, even if they are not physically here on Sunday? Wouldn't that be great?" He beamed at Cindy and gave her a thumbs up. "Good job, Cindy!" Then he turned and looked at the screen. "So please, if you know anyone on any of these teams, we've got middle school, high school, and even college. Please invite them to their corresponding Sunday, or any Sunday for that matter. You can even promise them gifts, if that will entice them." He laughed at his own joke, and then mock whispered into his microphone, "I'm not above bribing people to come to church." He laughed again, and a few of his congregants joined him.

He clapped his hands. "So let's get started! Today we have with us some members of the incredible Fort George Women's Basketball Team. If you ladies would like to join me up front, I promise not to make you feel too uncomfortable."

Chapter 28

hree Fort George basketball players stood in the front of the sanctuary: junior captain Ella, Madison, and Meghan. All three local girls.

Kyra watched them closely.

"Welcome to Greater Life, ladies," Darren said. "We're so glad you're here."

Brad slid his hand into hers again, interlocked their fingers, and squeezed. "This isn't so bad." His relief was audible.

"Not yet."

His chest shook with a silent chuckle, and she wanted to bury her head in that chest. She forced her eyes forward.

Darren turned his attention to his congregation. "It might be hard to believe looking at me now." He rubbed his bald head and laughed again. "But I was once a basketball player. So I know how hard these athletes work. Being good at basketball takes literally thousands of hours of sweat. It takes failing and trying again, falling down and getting up, hurting and healing." He looked at Kyra's players. "I absolutely admire you for what you've accomplished, and I'm sure many of these people here do too. Now, I know that Christians can be scary sometimes. We are ordinary people who are doing our best at life, and sometimes we make mistakes. But all Christians everywhere are one big family, often one big dysfunctional family, but a family nonetheless, and please know that you all are welcome to visit or join our family anytime. If there is ever anything you need, we hope you will call on us. We literally live to help others. So we're going to pray for you in a minute, but first, Cindy has some gifts. Cindy, would you come down?"

As Cindy popped up from the front row, Darren said, "These young women have a home game this Wednesday at seven o'clock. Please raise your hand if you're willing to attend that game and cheer them on."

Brad's free hand shot up. So did Cindy's. Kyra tried to be discreet as she counted hands. They fell quickly, but she saw at least five.

"Awesome! Thank you, brothers and sisters!"

Cindy had handed out three giant gift bags. They looked great. Blue and gold tissue paper spilled out of the top, and curly blue and gold ribbons sprang off the handles of the gold bags. Fort George's school colors. Kyra hadn't given Cindy enough credit.

"May I?" Cindy asked Darren.

May she what? Might be dangerous to give her carte blanche. She might start ordering parishioners to pair up and say wedding vows.

But Darren gave her permission.

"The gifts will change, depending on the age of the players," she said loudly, "but I just wanted to give you all an idea of what we're doing." She reached for Meghan's bag. "May I?"

A bewildered Meghan handed her bag back to Cindy.

To her credit, Cindy was gentle as she pulled a large box out of the bag and then set the bag on the floor. She opened the box and pulled out a large study Bible, which she held up for all to see. Appropriate oos and aahs erupted around her, and Kyra felt like she was at a baby shower. Then Cindy pulled out a folded blanket. It looked like one of those super soft snuggly ones, and Kyra was a little jealous. Cindy unfolded it and held it up in front of her. It had a giant basketball on it. She handed it to Meghan, still unfolded, and Kyra put a hand over her mouth to hide her laugh. Cindy was growing on her.

Cindy held up a book. "And this is a book of devotions for college athletes. There's also some candy and some info about our church."

She started repacking the bag as she talked. She even took the blanket back and refolded it. She handed the bag back to Meghan, who looked relieved. Then Cindy turned to face the congregation again. "If any of you want to help with this ministry, let me know."

"Great. Thank you, Cindy. Okay, let's pray!" Pastor Darren bowed his head.

Kyra bowed hers too, but she continued to watch her players. Meghan looked okay, but oh boy did the other two look uncomfortable. Kyra felt bad for them. This was probably a good idea, but still, she didn't like seeing her players so uneasy.

"Heavenly Father, we thank you for creating these awesome young women. We thank you for giving them the gifts and talents that you have given them. We thank you for instilling in them the work ethic it takes to develop those gifts and talents."

Kyra smiled at this sentiment. Maybe Pastor Darren wasn't *just* a pizza party pastor.

"We ask you to protect them in all their endeavors, especially when they are pushing themselves to train and compete. And above all, we ask that they be drawn closer to you now and throughout their lives. If there is a way for us as individuals or as a church to help them and bless them, please show us how. In Jesus' name we pray. Amen."

Ella's eyes popped open, and she looked less bewildered than she had before the prayer had started. So that was a good thing. Madison looked like she was standing on a tightrope over a pit of live spiders.

Darren dismissed them, and Kyra half expected them to leave the building, but none of them did. They all returned to their seats, and Meghan shocked her with a small smile before she sat down.

Darren stepped up to the platform and opened his Bible.

Kyra was hit with an unexpected wave of gratitude. For Cindy and her efforts, even if they didn't amount to much. For this church that had welcomed her when hers didn't. For Pastor Darren and his corny jokes and servant's heart. And for the high school computer teacher currently holding her hand.

Chapter 29

Cindy is pretty clever, Brad thought. But now what? They'd given them a Bible and prayed for them. Good things, for sure, but how were those good things going to help the woman beside him? Sure, God would speak through his children and through his Word, but that could easily be too little too late. He'd expected Cindy's grand plan to have more immediate effects.

He sighed and tried to focus on the sermon. He'd already missed who knows how much of it.

"Integrity means honesty, right?" Darren said from the pulpit. "People who have integrity do the right thing at the right time."

Oh boy, where were they? From the corner of his eye, he glanced at Kyra's Bible, which was open to Proverbs 10. Brad had made it to Proverbs, but that was as far as he'd gotten. He flipped to Chapter 10 and scanned the page for the word integrity.

"... those with integrity sacrifice immediate reward for the sake of justice," Darren said, "for the sake of goodness. You know, every spring our school, Freedom Academy ..." His eyes landed on one of the basketball players. "If you don't know, this church runs a small Christian school for K through 12. But anyone can go there. You don't have to go to this church to go there. Anyway, our school runs a spring field day. The student council does most of the work. Well, we had some senior cheaters last spring." He chuckled. "They didn't know that I knew, but I knew. I saw evidence that they were cheating. I was sad as these were good kids, kids who should have known better. Well, there were two seniors on the student council, and they caught on. Now, they had several choices in front of them. Honestly, I thought they would pretend that they hadn't noticed. That would have been the easiest choice. But you know what? That's not what they did. Instead, they simply didn't count the points that the cheating had gained their class." He paused to let those words settle.

"The cheating students noticed, started to complain, and the two student council reps stood firm and shook their heads, and the cheaters quieted down. I think it's worth noting that they didn't call them out in public, didn't humiliate them, because what good would have come from that? It would have left a sour note on the whole field day. Now, I don't know if they later rebuked them in private." He paused to chuckle. "All I know is what I saw in that moment. Those two student council leaders took a stand against their classmates. They did what was right. They chose to forgo the immediate reward of winning the field day, and they did it for the sake of justice, for the sake of goodness. The freshmen class won the field day. The seniors were disappointed, but there was very little drama. The truth won because of the integrity of two individuals who stood up to their friends." He paused again.

Brad's brain finally caught the connection between this story and Kyra's situation. A little late to the game, he was, but better late than never. He peeked at her to see if she'd caught on yet, but her face was impassive as usual.

"The World English Bible translation calls living with integrity *walking blamelessly*. Those two students were blameless in that situation. They had nothing to feel guilty about. They slept peacefully that night. The Bible goes on to say that those who walk with integrity walk *surely*. Isn't that a great word? Surely." He waited for agreement, which didn't audibly come.

"Well, I like that word. I remember a time when I was much younger, I went to an event in a city. I don't want to badmouth any city, so let's just leave it at that. It was a big city. Now, I was young, I wasn't walking with Jesus, and I was at an establishment I shouldn't have been at. Bad things were happening there, and I made some bad choices. There was some confusion, which often happens when people get together to make bad choices, and I ended up leaving alone and trying to walk back to my buddy's place, and I got turned around and well ... let's just say that before long I was fearing for my life. Every shadow was a threat. Every noise was dangerous. I knew that there were people nearby, crouching and waiting for a victim. I was certainly not walking surely." He stepped back from his Bible and put his hands in his pockets. The change in his pocket jingled.

"Now, I wasn't thinking of these verses from Proverbs back then, but I was living them out in real time. Had I not gone to that particular place and made those particular choices, had I been somewhere good and made good choices, I could have been walking surely, but I wasn't. That night, my steps were not sure. They were not safe. They were not comfortable because I had walked outside of integrity that night, and walking outside of integrity is dangerous. Now I didn't get mugged or murdered. Somehow, I found my way back to my buddy's apartment, and I lived to tell the story, but that hour it took me to find my way back? That hour was spent in sheer terror, and that fear was punishment enough. I don't ever want to feel like that again. If I'm ever walking somewhere dark and scary now, I want to know that I'm walking with God and that he's keeping me safe."

He stepped back to his Bible. "Almost done. Bear with me, I know you're getting hungry. The next line tells us that the person who 'perverts his ways will be found out.' Now, the word pervert brings to mind all sorts of unpleasant things, but the word simply means that someone has turned away from the right course, so someone who has turned away from walking with integrity *will be found out*. Will be found out." He didn't speak it like a threat. More like a sad truth. He gave the words some time to marinate.

"The truth is, family, that no one ever really gets away with anything. It may seem like people do. We may see the millionaire cheating and lying his way to wealth, and we may think he's getting away with it, but he is suffering in ways we can't see. And if he's not suffering, then he will be. Because we reap what we sow. And if we're sowing perversion, then we will reap a long, dark, walk through scary, dangerous territory. If we sow lies, we will reap fear. If we sow cheating, we will reap shame. If we sow manipulation, we will reap loneliness. Please hear me. I don't want you to suffer. I don't want you to have to live through the reaping of fear and shame and loneliness. I want God's very best for you, and the only way to get that is to walk upright. With integrity. With honesty. Even when it's inconvenient. Even when you have to stand up to those who want you to turn a blind eye. Even when it prevents you from getting some immediate reward. Choose integrity, friends. Reap a sure walk with your God. Let's pray."

Chapter 30

Kyra turned to walk down the center aisle and almost smacked into Ella.

"If I'd known this was your church, I wouldn't have come."

And even though she'd just enjoyed a week of snuggling up under God's wing, even though she'd just directly worshiped him for more than an hour, Kyra's response to this was immediate anger. "This isn't my church," she snapped. "My church kicked me out because they believed someone's lies." She instantly regretted her words. Ella wasn't a Christian, at least not to Kyra's knowledge, so Kyra shouldn't be making Christians look bad. Her mind scrambled for words to an apology.

"But you planned this, right?"

Kyra shook her head quickly. "I'm as surprised as you are." Well, maybe not quite as surprised, but close.

Ella studied her for a moment and then looked over her shoulder. "Hey, Meghan, get over here."

Grudgingly, Meghan came closer.

"If I call a team meeting and try to fix this, will you back me?"

Meghan's wide eyes flitted back and forth between Kyra and Ella. "Are you serious?"

Brad came closer too. Such an eavesdropper.

"Didn't you listen to all that?" Ella's tone was half joking, half serious.

"Yeah, but ..."

"But aren't you tired of all this? Aren't you tired of losing? We're partly to blame for all this because we're not fixing it."

Meghan stepped closer to Ella. "Maybe we should discuss this outside."

Ella gave her a dirty look. "Why? You don't have anything to be ashamed of. You didn't do anything."

"No, but she might have." She didn't need to specify who *she* was. They all knew she meant Kyra.

Ella barked out a laugh. "No, she didn't!"

"How do you know?"

"Are you serious?" Ella looked at Kyra and then back to Meghan. "You're serious. Um, no, the story's not true."

"But Charlotte has told me over and over that it is."

"That's because they were afraid you were going to tattle."

They? Who was they?

Meghan hung her head, obviously embarrassed.

Ella had no sympathy for her. "Are you going to back me or not?"

Kyra's mind was a storm of emotions. Was there hope? And did she want there to be? One of her captains had just admitted knowing it was a lie and not sticking up for her. Would a team meeting do anything?

Ella's body language expressed impatience at Meghan's lack of an answer.

"Sure. I guess," Meghan said.

"Good. Tomorrow morning. I'll set it up."

"Do you want me to do anything?" Kyra asked.

Ella looked her dead in the eyes. "Yeah. Stay out of it. I'll try to help, but I'm not doing this for you. This all happened because no one likes you."

The words knocked the wind out of her, and she took a step back.

"Now, wait a minute." Brad stepped in, obviously intent on defending her.

Kyra put her hand on his arm to try to stop him. She couldn't quite make herself speak.

"Sorry," Ella said. "Don't mean to be harsh, but it's no fun playing for a coach that hates you. Obviously, we're going to hate her back." She headed for the door with her head held high, her gift bag dangling from one long arm.

Watching her go, Kyra found her voice. "*That's* the one who's going to save me?"

Meghan was looking at Kyra. "I'm so sorry. Charlotte really did convince me. Either she's a good liar, or Ella is."

"I didn't do it," Kyra said for the zillionth time.

"Okay. Then I'm really, really sorry."

"It's okay, Meghan." And it really was. "This isn't your fault. I know you've been in a tough spot."

Without another word, Meghan followed Ella out of the sanctuary.

Kyra looked at Brad. "She didn't ride with you?"

He nodded. "She did. So I guess I should go take her home." He gave her arm a comforting squeeze.

"Hey, do you think Darren planned that message just for them?"

"I do not. We've been in Proverbs for weeks."

So God had probably planned it before any of this yogurt had ever hit the fan. That was comforting. "Okay. Talk to you soon."

He gave her small smile. "Have faith. I think the tide's about to turn."

January 31

Dear Frank,

I did it! I think my plan worked. Of course, even if it doesn't help Kyra, the plan will still work because it will reach people and bless people, but back to Kyra. I don't know for sure, but I thought I could see the wheels turning for one of those girls. She was listening to that sermon so intently. And then she went and talked to Kyra after church. I wanted to go listen to the conversation, but I showed restraint.

Anyway, just wanted to tell you about my small success. Wish you were here to celebrate with me. I have some leftover cake from Chanelle's baby shower. I think I'm going to go get some now and then turn in. Don't worry, I'll share with Bruno.

Love you,
Cindy

Chapter 31

K yra's phone rang at 10:20 on Monday morning.

"Hey. How are you doing?" Brad asked.

Enough with the pleasantries. They didn't have time for that! "Fine. What have you heard?"

He laughed. "So Meghan just called me with a report. It went well, but I didn't get many details. I figured you'd want to know right away, so I asked her to meet us."

"Us? Aren't you at work?"

"Yeah, but I've got lunch at five past eleven. If you can get here by then."

"Sure. Be right there." She hung up without thanking him, instantly regretted it, and then decided she didn't have time for regrets, just like she hadn't had time to thank him. She was still in her pajamas.

Kyra never went anywhere without looking her best, and she didn't have time to shower, do her hair, put on makeup, and drive to Freedom Academy before eleven.

Yet thirty minutes later, she'd impressed herself. The world's fastest shower, some dry shampoo, and less eyeliner than usual had done the trick. She checked herself in the mirror, winced, and then headed for the door.

Freedom Academy was buzzing with energy. She stepped into the lobby and looked around for Brad. Lots of people moved to and fro, but no Brad. She made her way to a sliding glass window. "I'm looking for Brad Foster?"

"Sure!" a friendly woman said and came toward the office door. "I'll take you right up." She looked at her empty hands. "Didn't you bring a lunch?"

Yeah right. Like she'd had time for that. She'd barely remembered her shoes. She shook her head.

"I'll get you something from the cafeteria." The woman led her up the stairs. "I'm Penny by the way. I'm the office manager."

"Nice to meet you. I'm Kyra."

She reached the top of the stairs and turned to smile at her. "Oh I know who you are. Right this way."

A bit bewildered, Kyra followed her down a narrow hallway to a doorway.

"Here he is!"

Kyra didn't know if she should knock. She looked to Penny for advice, but Penny was already scurrying away. Kyra softly rapped her knuckles on the door.

There was no answer, so she cracked the door open and peeked in. Brad and Meghan sat on opposite sides of a cluttered teacher's desk in the world's smallest computer room. Wall to wall tables held old desktop monitors. She closed the door behind her. She still couldn't believe he was a teacher. "So this is it, huh?" She looked around the cluttered space.

"Yep!" He leaned back in his chair and laced his fingers behind his head. "This is where I change lives."

Meghan laughed. "Oh, stop it."

"Come on in. Have a seat." He'd already moved an empty chair near his, and Kyra went to it. An untouched sandwich sat on his desk.

Kyra sat and looked at Meghan expectantly. Meghan had no food either.

"So, one more time, I'm really sorry. I know I've been an idiot about this whole thing."

"It's okay," Kyra said quickly. The suspense was killing her.

"So, you know Ella is crazy popular, right?" Meghan said.

Brad's classroom door burst open, and a boy threw himself through it, then stopped quick and looked at Brad's visitors with wide eyes.

"What's wrong, Caleb?"

Caleb stared at Kyra and sniffed. He'd been crying. "Never mind."

"No, no, come on in. These are friends of mine. They're safe."

Caleb crept closer. "I was just hoping I could hide in here."

"It's happening again?"

He nodded.

"Did you already get something to eat?"

He shook his head.

Brad popped up, went around his desk, and put his arm around the young boy's shoulders. "Come on. Let's go get you some lunch." He looked at Kyra. "Be right back." Then he left her alone with Meghan, who busied herself studying her right shoe.

It took a long time, but Brad did come back.

"Sorry about that." He sat down in his chair.

"Is he being bullied?" Meghan asked.

Brad nodded. "'Fraid so."

"At a Christian school?"

"Christians can be bullies too. In fact, they can be quite good at it." He looked at Meghan. "Okay, you were telling us about how popular Ella is."

"And he came to you?" Kyra interrupted. "Does he hide out in here a lot?"

"Not a lot. But some. A few kids do."

Kyra was impressed. She'd never had a high school classroom she could run to like some kind of fortress.

"Okay," Brad said. "Ella."

Meghan nodded. "Right. Wicked popular. I've never really understood that because she's kind of a—" She stopped herself from swearing.

"What happened?" Brad prodded.

"So she didn't invite Charlotte or Avery to the meeting."

Interesting.

"But they showed up anyway. Someone told them. And it turned into a big fight. Charlotte's people against Ella's people."

"Oh." Kyra wished someone had taped it.

"But Ella called them out. Said that their lies were stupid, that all that they were accomplishing was turning us into a losing team, that they weren't even getting more playing time."

"*That's* why they did this?" Brad sounded horrified.

"Well, everyone's mad that we have out-of-staters playing ahead of people from around here."

"The out-of-staters are better," Kyra said. "That's why we win."

Brad gave her a look that said, *Seriously? You need to point that out now?*

"I know that," Meghan snapped. Then she softened her tone to add, "Doesn't mean we like it. Charlotte used to be a starter before you got here." She took a big breath. "Anyway, Ella basically said, 'Your plan was stupid, it didn't work, we're still not playing, and now we're losing. You didn't even get her fired. All you did was embarrass all of us.'"

"And?" Brad said. "What did they say?"

"Not much. But Ella said, 'I called this meeting to say that I'm going to Mr. Basso with the truth. And I think you all should come with me. But now that you ...' She meant Charlotte and Avery. 'Now that you are here, I think you should come clean.' And Charlotte was like, 'What? And get kicked off the team? No way!' and then Saylor jumped in and sided with them, and it came out that this whole thing had been Saylor's idea."

Breath rushed out Kyra as understanding washed over her. "Saylor was smart enough not to do the accusing herself. She made someone else do it."

Meghan nodded. "Right. She doesn't want to embarrass herself, ever. But she convinced Charlotte that she could get you fired and get her team back. Then she got impatient, so she told Avery to join the fun. Anyway, Saylor was freaking out, and Ella said, 'Don't act like you did this for our local girls. This is about Jen!'"

And there it was. Kyra looked at Brad. "The one I booted for Adderall."

"I remember." He didn't take his eyes off Meghan. "Is Ella still going to the AD?"

Meghan nodded. "We did it right after the meeting. Most of us. Turns out that only Saylor, Charlotte, Avery, and Madison knew the plan at first. But now Madison is on Ella's side."

Wow. Madison had been in church. Cindy's plan had worked.

"And what did Mr. Basso say?" Brad pressed.

"Not much. He thanked us for our honesty and said he would look into it."

Kyra looked at Brad. "That's it? I have to go see him."

"Hang on a sec. Anything else?"

The classroom door opened, and Penny came in with a tray. "Sorry, it's not much, but our mac and cheese is pretty good."

Kyra tried to be gracious as she thanked her. Then as soon as Penny left the room, she set her tray on Brad's desk.

Meghan eyed it. "Are you going to eat that?"

Kyra swept her hand at it. "Be my guest." Great. Now she would have to get the rest of the scoop around mac and cheese bites.

"What else, Meghan?" Brad tried to refocus her.

She shook her head. "That's it, I think."

"How did Ella know?" Kyra asked.

"Know what?"

Kyra tried not to show her impatience. "How did Ella know it was a plan? She wasn't in on it, right? So how did she know that they were lying?"

"Right. I guess Saylor got drunk and confided in her." She slapped a hand over her mouth, and her eyes grew wide.

Brad rolled his eyes.

"They were right," Meghan said after she slowly lowered her hand. "I am a tattletale."

"Not really," Brad said. "It's hard to keep so many secrets." He looked at Kyra. "What a bunch of hellions. I'm so sorry."

Chapter 32

Brad followed Kyra out of his classroom. He knew she was going to go straight to her boss, and he was worried about her next steps. He caught her arm.

She stopped and turned to face him, and again he was struck by her beauty.

He let go of her arm. "What are you going to do?"

"I'm going to get my job back and then kick Charlotte and Avery off the team. Saylor too, if I can swing it. But I promise not to throw Meghan under the bus for the booze tattling." She shook her head. "I can't believe Saylor is drinking during the season. I knew she was a brat, but I also thought she was a serious athlete."

"If you kick three girls off the team, how many will you have left?"

"Enough."

"Will you still be able to win?" He could care less about her answer. He only wanted her to think before leaping.

She folded her arms across her chest. "I thought you said winning wasn't the most important thing."

Ah, nice. How he loved having his words thrown back in his face. "It's not, but ..." He scratched his head, trying to come up with the right words. "I was trying to get you to reconsider—"

"Reconsider?" she cried too loudly. "You want me to reconsider what, exactly? You think I should keep Charlotte on the team? She should go to jail for what she did!"

He didn't know about that. She'd done a bad thing, sure, but jail time? *Come on, now.* "I just think you might want to slow your roll a little—"

"Slow your roll?" she said with a smirk. "You're so hip, hanging out with all these teens."

He frowned. "I think that's a millennial expression, actually."

Her brow furrowed. "So?"

"So ..." He waved his arm toward the ruckus coming from the busy cafeteria. "These guys are Gen Z."

She rolled her eyes. "Whatever. Anything else?"

Now he was annoyed. Being Kyra's friend was a roller coaster. "Yes. There's something else. Grace. Love. Forgiveness. You know, all the things Jesus gives us and wants us to regift to others. You might consider them."

"You're right."

He sighed with relief.

His relief was short-lived.

"I'll forgive them because God has forgiven me. But I'm going to kick them off my team first." She turned to go, but then whirled back to him, making him a bit dizzy. She planted a firm, awesome kiss on his cheek, and the smell of wild roses washed over him. She pulled back a few inches and smiled at him. He was dazzled. "Thank you," she whispered. "You are my favorite person ever."

He couldn't help but smile back even though he was still annoyed with her Old Testament wrath. "You're welcome. And ditto." He watched her walk away and then returned to his sandwich.

Meghan was polishing off her free mac and cheese. "Okay, so she's not a perve who sleeps with her students, but I still don't know why you're so in love with her."

Brad gazed in the direction she'd gone. "Is it that obvious?"

Meghan laughed. "Yes."

He sat down and picked up his sandwich.

"But really, why?"

She actually wanted to know? He sighed. "I don't know. Because she's beautiful. Because she's smart. Confident. Good at what she does. I admire her. But I also feel this strong need to take care of her—"

"Oh no"—she stretched *no* into three syllables—"sorry I asked!" She put the tray on his desk and stood. "I've got to get back. But I really am sorry that I didn't help sooner." She let out a small, uncomfortable laugh. "Or at all really. I do regret that."

"I know." He took a bite of his ham and cheese on rye.

"So you're not mad at me?" she asked sweetly.

He shook his head and said through a mouthful, "Of course not. You're you." He smiled. He thought probably she could make him angry if she tried hard enough, but he knew he'd never stay mad at her. She might not be his niece exactly, but he certainly loved her like one.

She returned his smile and then bounced out of his room.

He glanced at the clock. He had about one and half minutes to finish his sandwich before his room was flooded with youngsters who specialized in getting computer programs to crash. He chewed faster, hoping Kyra didn't march into her boss's office and make things worse.

He was out of time, and his sandwich was too dry to choke down quickly. He could hear them coming. He dropped the rest of his lunch in the trash and got ready for the stampede.

Chapter 33

"What do you mean it's not enough?" Kyra cried. She couldn't believe her ears.

"Have a seat." Dave pointed to a chair.

Kyra didn't want to sit. She did, though.

"Now it's the word of two girls against the word of seven girls. If I didn't believe you, then their grand gesture of stomping in here would have gone a long way to convincing me, but I do believe you, always have, so their gesture accomplished very little."

She caught him eying her hands, realized they were clenched into tight fists, and forced herself to relax them.

"I'm glad they came in. Don't get me wrong. It was a good thing. But I still need to work things out with the powers that be. And it's going to take time, especially if your two accusers stick to their story."

"But have you told the higherups about the seven girls?"

"I will. And Kyra, that's not all you have going for you. I've built a timeline, and these girls cannot name a single time that they were alone with you. They're not even trying because they know we'll be able to prove that they weren't. This is going to work out the way it's supposed to. I just need a little more time."

"I should talk to Ella again. Maybe she can push—"

"You should not talk to Ella again. She's done what she should do, what she could do. You need to stop trying to control everything and let me do my job." Now he sounded annoyed.

"Sorry."

"No worries. I know this isn't easy for you, but I promise, I'm doing a good job at fixing it. But nothing real is instant."

She smiled.

"What?"

"I like that saying. I haven't heard it before."

"I don't think it's a saying. I think I made it up."

She stood. "Even better. May I use it? I'll give you credit."

He waved an arm at her. "Be my guest. And before you go, have you decided how you're going to handle coming back?"

She stared at him, not understanding his question.

"I mean, while you've got time, maybe you should think about your next steps. Do you plan on disciplining any of the girls? If so, who? And what?"

She hesitated. These weren't hard questions, and yet, she didn't have the answers. Brad's voice echoed in her heart: grace, love, forgiveness.

She couldn't answer the question, so she dodged it. "Did they tell you that Saylor was the one who came up with the plan?"

He nodded. "And they told me why." He was still waiting for an answer.

She sighed. "I guess I don't know yet. It depends on whether or not they come clean. Sticking to their lie even if I get reinstated is a lot different than apologizing to me."

"So you want an apology?"

"Of course. Don't you?"

He studied her.

What was he getting at? What did he want her to say? "I guess that my official answer is that I don't know yet, but I'm probably not going to kick them all off the team or anything."

His eyebrows flew up. "Really?"

His shock offended her a little. "Really. Is that so hard to believe?"

He chuckled. "A little, yeah. But I'm not upset to hear it."

"Why's that?"

He seemed to be struggling to decide whether to answer her. Finally, he said, "Kyra, would you mind sitting for another minute?"

Her stomach rolled. This wasn't good, she could tell already. But she sat.

"Please don't take this as a criticism. It's not. You are a great coach. I hired you because I believed that, and I hired you for a second season because you proved it to be true. You know the game, and you get results. But ..." Now he was considering whether to continue.

He decided to. "I think this happened because of how disliked you are." He held up both hands. "I'm not saying that coaches need to be liked. I don't think that's true. But I do wonder if you might have a more successful career if you tried to be ... a tiny bit more ..."

She had no idea how he was going to end that sentence.

"Nice."

"Nice?"

"Yeah. Nice. I'm not saying to coddle them. I don't want you trying to win a popularity contest. But yeah, a little nicer. Hollering at them might be a little more effective if you balance it with a little praise."

She did praise them. When they did something praiseworthy. But that rarely happened. "Okay." She didn't know what else to say.

He smiled. "Okay."

She started to get up but then had another thought. "When I was a kid, I had this favorite book. I must have read it five times. I still have a worn-out copy somewhere. It's probably out of print now, but it was such a good book. Anyway, it was called *The Coach Nobody Liked*, and it was about this really tough coach who came into town and whipped the boys into shape. At first the main character didn't like it, he was one of the players, but then once he was successful, he appreciated that coach for doing his job." She couldn't read the wry smile on his face. "What?"

"John F. Carson. I loved that book. Had forgotten all about it." He leaned forward. "But you know what I remember about that book?"

She shook her head.

"The father in that book ... *he* was the one who insisted on a win-at-all-costs philosophy. It was the coach who taught the boys that basketball was about more than winning."

Her body went cold. She didn't remember it like that at all. But it had been a long time since she'd read it. "Sorry," she said weakly. She wanted to get out of there. She was embarrassed.

"Don't be. I'm impressed that you've read it. It's a pretty obscure book." He smiled. "You're young, Kyra. You're still figuring this all out. And if you keep trying to figure it out, if you don't suddenly think that you've arrived, well, then you'll keep getting better and better. And if you're already this good a coach, just imagine how good you'll one day be." He laughed. "I'm not naive enough to think that you'll still be here when you reach that level. I know we're just a rung on your ladder. But I will be your fan wherever you end up, Kyra Carter."

Chapter 34

Kyra watched the basketball game on her phone screen. Brad was such a hero for keeping up with this ridiculous filming. She knew he wasn't enjoying it, and she thanked him every five minutes. He rarely replied, of course, because he didn't want to be seen talking to himself in the bleachers.

Her team was playing well. They were up by eight points. Saylor had been benched. Even with her tiny viewing window, she could tell Saylor was unhappy about that decision. Good job, Dave.

The buzzer sounded, declaring it halftime, and Brad asked for a break. He said he needed to get a snack and didn't want her to hear him chewing.

"Sure, go ahead. I don't want you to die of starvation during the second half." She sank back into her couch to twiddle her thumbs and wait.

Her mind drifted back to that old favorite novel. She'd reread it since talking to Dave, and he'd been right. The father had been the one who insisted on winning—not the good coach.

How had she gotten that so wrong? Had her young mind lumped that fictional father in with her real father? It would have been easy enough to do. Because that's who her father was, wasn't it? Sure, he'd mellowed some with age, but that was still who he was.

And it certainly had been who he was back then. He'd coached her in middle school, and if they lost a game—certainly if they lost because of something she'd done wrong—he would berate her all the way home.

Her breath caught. What was this line of thinking? She never thought about her father like this. And why not? It was how he was. It was the truth.

Of course, she'd always known that she got her competitive spirit from him, but this was the first time she'd ever considered that might not be entirely a good thing.

He had pushed her. Always. To be her best. To win. To not make mistakes.

And when she had made mistakes, there hadn't been a whole lot of ... what had been on Brad's list? Grace. Forgiveness. Love.

Of course he loved me, she thought. A father loves his children. And yes, he had loved her. But if she was completely honest ... she squeezed her eyes shut and forced herself to focus on the idea, to face it: If she was completely honest, in those moments immediately following those mistakes, it had sure seemed like he hit pause on that love.

It had sure seemed like he only loved her when she *wasn't* making mistakes. When she was winning.

Her eyes filled with tears, and she swatted them away. This was crazy. She didn't need to be crying about her childhood. She had enjoyed a good childhood. A healthy, supportive childhood. She'd been a pastor's kid for crying out loud. She'd had an awesome stepmother.

But the tears still came. Because it was true. And because she'd never seen it before.

Some part of her had always believed she was only loved when she was doing things right. She knew that wasn't true. She knew her father loved her, but that belief—well, sometimes people believe things even when their rational brains know otherwise.

Her phone rang, and she grabbed it.

"Ready for round two?"

She took a breath, glad Brad couldn't see her. "Sure am."

"Are you okay?"

"Yes. Sorry. Got something stuck in my throat." This wasn't a lie. There was a golfball-sized lump in her throat.

The basketball court appeared on her phone, and her girls strode out onto the floor. Saylor was still on the bench.

The ref handed Daphne the ball and blew the whistle, and Daphne inbounded it. Kyra's eyes followed the ball up and down the court, but her mind was still on her father. She wasn't mad at him. She couldn't be. She understood why he'd operated like that. A pastor's family lives in a fishbowl. Someone is always watching, always judging, so of course he cared about what people thought. His ministry, not to mention his livelihood, depended on it.

But still. Something had gotten lost in translation, hadn't it?

And she was only just figuring this out when she was thirty? How was that?

The answer hit her with a slap: she'd finally slowed down enough to figure it out.

She'd been running as hard as she could to be as good as she could be for as long as she could remember. These last few weeks, she'd pretty much come to a screeching halt.

And then there was Brad.

Brad, who saw the world so differently than she did, who saw God so differently.

She gasped.

Had she somehow conflated her two fathers? If she'd grown up thinking she had to earn her father's love, did she also think she had to earn God's love?

No. That was silly. She knew that God's love was unconditional. She'd been taught that since birth.

And yet ... there was something there. Something perched right on the edge of her understanding. Part of her desperately wanted to talk to Brad about it. He would be able to help her process all of it. But the other part of her wanted to go back to life before any of this confusion had dawned.

"Congratulations," Brad said.

"For what?"

He snickered. "For winning, silly."

Oh. Of course. "Thanks. I didn't do much, though."

"Not true. That's still your team. Your offense. Your plays. Your training."

"Thank you."

"Okay to shut the camera off?"

"Yeah, of course."

The video cut out.

"Hey, are you sure you're okay?" She could hear that he was moving. Probably making a beeline for the door.

"Yeah, sorry. Just tired." This was not a lie.

"Okay. I just thought you'd be more excited. You guys finally won one."

"I am excited." *That* was a lie. And why wasn't she excited? She didn't know.

"Hey, you're not worried that they just proved that they can do it without you, are you?"

She chuckled. "Honestly, that hadn't occurred to me. I'm happy, honest." She didn't want to talk about it anymore. "And thank you for filming."

"You already thanked me for that."

"Not since the first half."

He laughed. "Well, you're welcome."

"Okay, well, have a good night." She wanted to see him, but it was late, and she really was tired.

"You too."

They said goodbye, and she hung up. What was she going to do about Brad? She liked him an awful lot. It was more than attraction. She didn't know quite what it was yet, but it was a lot more than attraction.

Chapter 35

Kyra's phone rang at nine o'clock in the morning. Her caller ID said Dave. She hurried to answer.

"Good morning. I've got good news. Can you come in?"

"Sure. And hey, thanks for winning last night." If that was the good news he wanted her to come in to hear, she wanted him to know she was already aware.

"You're welcome. See you soon."

She didn't know whether to be nervous or hopeful. She trusted Dave; if he told her it was good news, then it would be. So why was her gut tight with dread? *Father, take control of this situation,* she prayed on her way out the door. Then she laughed.

He was already in control of the situation. Why did she have so much trouble remembering that?

She caught herself speeding on the icy Hartport roads and pulled her foot off the gas. Seconds later, she met a cop car. *Thank you, Father.* She really couldn't afford a speeding ticket right now. Especially since she still feared the imminent cancellation of her modest salary.

The field house's parking lot wasn't empty, but it was close. This was good. She wasn't feeling very social.

As she walked down the hallway, she glanced longingly at her office door. She couldn't wait to get back in there. It felt more like home than her house did. But she veered off and went into her boss's office instead.

"Good morning!" Oh indeed, he was feeling bouncy today. He jumped up and shut the door behind her, sweeping a hand toward a chair. "Come on in."

Gingerly, she sat.

He eyed her. "You okay?"

"I am. Just waiting for the other shoe to drop."

He laughed and sat. "I told you it was good news."

"I know. Can't help but be a little paranoid, though."

"Nope. Don't be paranoid. I'd like you to come back to work today, if you're up for it."

It felt like her head detached from her body and was just floating there above her. "Really?"

He nodded, smiling. "I thought you'd like that. I'll take some of the credit, but a lot of it goes to Ella Hall. Last night after the game, Avery came in here and told me the whole story. She admitted that she lied, and she said that Charlotte was lying too. Charlotte still hasn't confessed, but I've talked to administration, and they're letting me make the decision. So, I'm bringing you back. If you want to come back." She wasn't sure how he wanted her to answer that, but she nodded. He smiled. "Good. Now, how do you want to handle things? Avery has already quit, so you don't have to kick her off the team, but Charlotte and Saylor are another—"

"Quit? Oh sorry." She hadn't meant to interrupt. But she'd quit?

He nodded. "She was pretty embarrassed."

Good. She should be. An unpleasant theory popped into her head. "Do you think Ella is pressuring her into quitting?" He'd said that Ella should get some credit, but he hadn't said why. What had Ella done, exactly?

"I don't think so. The Ella part of the story is pretty strange. Avery said that Ella came to her in private and talked to her about integrity and reaping what you sow."

Kyra bit the inside of her cheek.

"Apparently Ella went to Charlotte with the same speech, but it didn't have the same effect on her."

"Wow." She couldn't think of any other words. Her wheels were spinning in place trying to process.

"Yes. Wow." Maybe his wheels were spinning too. "It's a little sticky because this whole scheme was Saylor's idea, but we can't prove that. Doesn't mean you can't boot her, though. Or bench her." He shrugged and then waited for her to speak.

Slowly she said, "I don't think I'm going to boot or bench anyone. And can you get Avery back in here to talk to me today? Before practice?"

"You're not?" He ignored her second question.

"I don't think so. Not yet anyway."

"Do you mind if I ask why not?"

She took a deep breath. Her rational brain didn't know why not. She just felt like that was the right thing to do. "I think I'm going to choose grace."

"Grace."

She nodded. "Grace. Another chance. They did a horrible thing, but I'm not sure what good it would do them to boot them."

"What good it would do them?" Was he going to repeat everything she said? "You know, Kyra, in this situation, it wouldn't be out of line to think about what good these decisions would do *you*."

Still. Something inside her resisted such a definitive response. "Thank you for your support, but I think I'd like to get everyone back on the team. I think I'd like to try again."

"Everyone?"

She remembered Jen. It hadn't even occurred to her to give Jen a second chance. But maybe she should.

If she let Jen back on the team, did that mean she'd let Saylor win? Maybe. But did it matter who won this stupid battle that no one of import was even paying attention to?

"Sure. Why not. Everyone's invited back for another chance."

His eyes narrowed as he studied her. "Wow. What got into you?"

Brad, maybe? God, maybe? Time to think? "I don't know. Maybe I'm growing."

He chuckled. "Oh, you're definitely growing. And it's very cool to watch." He waved her toward the door. "Get back to work. You've got a season to save. I'll set up a meeting with Avery."

Chapter 36

K yra was so glad to be back in her office that she was getting very little done. She'd already called Brad and filled him in. She asked him to tell Darren and Cindy. She figured that Meghan already knew. And now she was busy enjoying the feel of her carpet on her feet; the smell of the place: leather and old books; and the sight of her walls.

It was good to be home.

Finally she got around to planning her first practice back and was interrupted by a soft tapping on the door.

"Come in!" she called.

The door opened a crack, and Kyra caught a glimpse of a bashful Avery.

"Come on in."

Slowly the door opened, and Avery stepped inside.

"Have a seat."

It was frustrating how slowly she moved, but Kyra couldn't imagine all that she was feeling.

She finally found her way into the chair.

"Mr. Basso tells me that you've quit my team?"

She wouldn't meet her eyes.

"I wish you wouldn't."

Now she looked up. "What? Why?"

"We've got to put this behind us, Avery. You've got to put it behind you. I've got to put it behind me. Charlotte and Saylor will have to do the same thing eventually, when they're ready. Wouldn't it be better to try to heal together than to just run away?"

Avery stared at her. "Don't you hate me?"

Almost.

Maybe not. It wasn't hatred. It was anger. It was horror. It was a sick feeling she got when she looked at her.

But it wasn't hatred. "I don't hate you."

"I'm really sorry."

"I know."

She rubbed her face. "I don't even know why I did it. I was mad I wasn't getting any playing time. I went from high school star to bench-warmer getting screamed at, and I ... Saylor made it sound like such a good plan. But it didn't work. You didn't get fired. I didn't get played. And now the whole school thinks I'm a lesbian." Her voice cracked. "And a liar."

Kyra didn't know what to say. "I forgive you, Avery." The words surprised her. The truth of them surprised her even more. "Come back on my team. Work hard. Let's get back into the playoffs."

She considered it. "I don't know if I can. Are Saylor and Charlotte on the team still?"

"As far as I know. But I'll protect you. Ella will protect you."

"Can I think about it?"

This new burst of compassion was running low. "You have till practice. If you're not there today ready to go, then I'll assume you've decided not to continue with your team."

She nodded and got up. She went to the door, paused with her hand on the knob, and said, "Thank you."

"You're welcome. See you in a few hours." She hoped.

Ella showed up twenty minutes later, banging on her door and then opening it without permission. "Can I talk to you?"

"Sure. Come on in."

"Good." She shut the door behind her. "Because I skipped class for this."

"I really don't want you skipping class, Ella."

"I know." She fell into a chair. It was hard to believe this girl had any athleticism at all, but she did. "We have a problem."

"A new one?"

She laughed.

"Thank you, by the way, for all you've done."

"You're welcome. But I didn't do it for you."

"I know. So what's the problem?"

"We are away this weekend."

"I'm aware."

"So girls are freaking out about motel arrangements."

Oh for crying out loud. "Already?"

"Yeah. Your team is split right down the middle. Well, one side is bigger than the other, but still split."

Kyra didn't know which side was bigger, but she didn't have the energy to analyze it. She let out a long breath. In the past, Kyra had been a control freak about assigning roommates. She abhorred cliques and tried to prevent them from forming. "Can you do me a favor, Captain?" It would be the first real leadership duty that she'd asked of the young woman.

"Want me to organize the rooms?"

She chuckled. "Yes. I'm not promising I'll follow your suggestions, but you obviously have a finger on the pulse of this team more than I do. I don't even know if you can find a way to make everyone feel safe, but if you could, I'd like to hear it."

"Sure, no prob." She pushed herself out of the chair. "Thanks."

"Of course."

"You know, there are rumors that Saylor's quitting."

She was tempted to say, *Good.* "Well, I'll deal with that bridge if we get there."

"Okay. Just wanted to warn you."

Kyra looked at her captain. "Warning heeded. Get to class."

Chapter 37

Kyra stepped into the gym five minutes before practice was supposed to start. Sure enough, the girls were split. Charlotte, Avery, and Madison shot on one hoop. The rest shot at the other.

No sign of Saylor.

"Welcome back." Coach Weiger came and gave her a loose hug. After she'd let go and stepped back, she said in a low voice, "I owe you an apology."

"Don't mention it." She didn't want to talk about it. She had bigger things to think about.

"I need to."

Kyra looked at her.

"If you don't mind."

Kyra gestured at her to go ahead.

"I should have stuck up for you, and I didn't. I'm sorry. I was worried about losing my own job, and I'm sorry."

It was more than that. Weiger was more than ready to step into Kyra's head coaching shoes. The fact that Dave hadn't made her the interim head coach should have told her that was never going to happen, but jealousy is a hard beast to reason with. "You're forgiven."

Kyra called the girls in, and they bunched up in a loose huddle in front of her, staring at her expectantly.

She'd been trying for the last hour to write this speech, and though she was good at pep talks, she had come up with very little for this one.

"We have four games left. We need to win all four to make the play-offs." She gave that a few seconds to sink in. "I would like to make the playoffs. Would any of you like to make the playoffs?"

Most of them nodded. Charlotte stared at her with cold eyes. Avery looked at the floor.

"I don't want to embarrass Avery, but I want her teammates to know that she has apologized to me, and I have completely forgiven her. And I'm asking you all to forgive her too. She made a mistake, but mistakes aren't the end of the world."

She paused to relish her own words. What a novel thought. Mistakes weren't the end of the world. She needed to write that down.

"I'm also asking you all to forgive Charlotte."

Charlotte narrowed her eyes.

"As I have done."

"We're not going to win without Saylor," Charlotte said.

"I disagree."

Movement from the doorway caught Kyra's eye. She looked up, and her team turned to follow her gaze. Jennifer Lane had just stepped into the gym, all dressed and ready to go. "Sorry I'm late," she said. "I just got your message."

"Come on in," Kyra said. Then she looked at her team. "Jen made a mistake too. But since this seems to be the season for second chances, I've invited her to join us for the rest of the season."

Ella jumped up and down and then tackled Jen in a hug. With her arm around her shoulders, she pulled her into the huddle. "This sure will help with the whole winning thing."

Kyra smiled. Ella was really growing on her. She was starting to see how she'd gotten so many captain votes.

"So let's warm up. Then we're going to work on our new offense."

"New offense?"

"Don't worry. It's a lot like the old one." But this one would work without Saylor.

She watched them go through their warmups, and it was almost as if things were back to normal. After warmups, she ran them through a few routine drills and then they started reviewing the new offense, and things almost seemed better than normal. Girls were more attentive. They were hustling more. No one was snarky. Interesting.

After she dismissed them, she caught Ella's eye. "You all were unusually cooperative today."

Ella nodded. "I noticed that. I think that in a way, we missed you. I mean, I don't want to admit it, but I think it might be true. And you didn't holler at anyone today. Usually that puts us in a bad mood, but you didn't do it." She slapped her on the back, a gesture far too familiar for Kyra's tastes, but she tried not to respond. "Good job, Coach!" Ella laughed and trotted off.

Weiger was staring at her. "It's true. I know you have to holler at them sometimes, and I'm not saying you shouldn't. But the whole mood today was different. Sometimes it feels kind of fear-based, like they're doing their best so they don't get in trouble. Today was different. I'm not sure what their motivation was, but I don't think fear was involved."

Chapter 38

"Want to celebrate?"

Brad read Kyra's text with mixed emotions. Yes, he definitely wanted to see her. Of course he did. But he'd received her good news with mixed emotions. Of course he was glad she'd won the battle. Her name had been cleared. She'd gotten her job back.

But he also knew that this meant she was back on the ladder.

It was silly, really. Even if she'd gotten fired, she would have moved on soon. But some small foolish part of him had let himself believe that she might stick around. She'd needed him. Maybe she'd come to love him too.

Now she didn't need him. Now she might forget all about him. "Sure," he typed. "What do you want to do?"

"Well …"

He waited impatiently for her to say more.

"I'm worried you might be sick of Mexican."

"Never." He'd already eaten supper, but he'd never tell her that.

She sent him a laughing emoji. "Great. It's a date then."

Was it? Was it really a date? "When do you want to go?"

"I'm ready when you are."

He put on a clean shirt, checked himself in the mirror, and headed for the door.

On the short drive to her house, he tried to psych himself up. Maybe there was still a chance. She'd reached out to him. She'd asked him to hang out. Maybe she had real feelings for him.

Or maybe this was her saying goodbye.

No, not yet. She still had a few weeks of basketball left.

That's why the first question he asked her when they sat down was, "Does your salary match the school year?"

She laughed. "What?"

She was right. That hadn't made sense. "I mean, I know you get paid for the basketball season." He might as well come right out with it. "I was wondering if you planned to move on as soon as the season's over or if you're expected to finish the school year."

"Oh." Her face fell. "Well, I haven't really thought about leaving yet."

He didn't believe her.

"But yeah, I am expected to finish the year. I mean I don't have to, but yeah, I'd lose some of my yearly salary if I left sooner than that."

Good. So maybe she'd stick around for spring at least. "Did you hang out here last summer?"

She nodded. "Of course. I do a lot of recruiting in the summer." She did? His surprise must have shown because she explained, "Some seniors don't get the offers they think they're going to get from bigger schools. So I come along and try to scoop them up. I also get a head start on good juniors."

His mind drifted. He was getting sick of basketball. Watching it. Talking about it. Thinking about it. He was glad they were going to play away this weekend so he wouldn't be expected to go. By Kyra or Meghan.

The server came and took their drink order.

"Ginger ale?" She asked as soon as he was out of earshot. "Have you aged thirty years since we've last talked?"

He didn't get the joke. Did old people drink ginger ale?

"Sorry. Yet another failed joke. Maybe I should stop trying to be funny."

He forced a smile. "Please don't. I think you're funny. Sometimes."

She giggled, and it was the lightest, airiest sound he'd heard come out of her.

He realized then that he didn't even know her. Not really. He only knew the worried, desperate version. Maybe he wouldn't even like the version of her that wasn't in trouble. He found himself wishing that would be the case. That would be safest.

"Wow, you are a million miles away tonight."

"Sorry." He rubbed his stomach. "Not feeling the greatest."

"Oh, I'm sorry."

"So, how was practice?"

"It was really good! I think you'll be proud of me."

He smiled. She had no idea how proud he was of her, how proud he was to know her, to be part of her life. "What happened?"

"Well, for starters, I didn't kick anyone off the team." Her smile was so bright, he felt like a deer in headlights.

He couldn't look away. "That's good. Very gracious of you."

"Even Jennifer."

It took him a second to register who Jennifer was. "Oh wow! She came back?"

Kyra beamed at him. "She did!"

He knew he was gawking at her, but he couldn't help it. That sparkle in her eye. That wide, wide grin.

"What?" she asked, self-conscious.

He shook his head. "I've just never seen you this happy. It's ... beautiful."

Pink rose in her tan cheeks. Her makeup tried to hide it but couldn't quite mask it all. "I am happy, and that's partly thanks to you."

Now it was his turn for warm cheeks. "Only partly?"

She laughed.

Their sodas came, and she downed half of hers immediately.

"Thirsty?"

"Yes. And hungry." She looked longingly at the swinging kitchen door.

"Shouldn't be too long. They're always pretty fast."

"I know." She turned her eyes on him. "But really, though. Thank you for helping me to see God, and life for that matter, from a different angle."

"Oh yeah? Has that happened?"

"I think it's still happening. I mean, I've always been a believer, but I've spent more time with God this last week than ... well, I don't know. But really concentrating on him, well, it makes life seem more ..."

"Peaceful?" he offered as she said, "Manageable." She laughed. "And peaceful too. I don't know if it's your voice, your church's culture, or the Bible itself, but some new ideas have been sprouting in my brain."

"Oh yeah?" New ideas like spending the rest of her life in Hartport? "Like what?"

"Like maybe I haven't been really living in God's unconditional love. I mean ... that's not quite what I meant. Let me try again. My brain has always known that God's love is unconditional, but I wasn't living like I knew that." She pretended to slap herself in the forehead. "Sorry, I sound like an imbecile, but these realizations feel really profound on the inside."

He smiled. "I think I understand." He didn't know how to put it into words either. But he knew it was a good thing. He could see its goodness all over her.

Chapter 39

Kyra was almost sad when Brad pulled his car into her driveway. She wasn't ready for the evening to end.

"Can I walk you to your door?" Brad asked.

With the wind chill, it was about twenty below out, so Kyra felt bad saying yes, but she did want him to walk her to her door. She wanted him to kiss her good night. She couldn't believe they'd spent this much time together and he hadn't given her a real kiss yet. Granted, she hadn't initiated one either. She'd had too much other stuff to think about. But now that the crisis was pretty much over, she really, really wanted to kiss him.

"Yes. Please."

She couldn't read his face in the dark, but he got out and came around to her side of the car and took her hand. His hand felt so warm, she didn't want him to let go.

They reached the door. She didn't want to give things a chance to get awkward, so she turned and pressed her lips to his.

He immediately pulled away.

Well, that hadn't gone the way she'd thought it would. And all of the joy she'd been carrying around all day zipped out of her like air from a punctured balloon. "Sorry," she said. And she was sorry. She was sorry she'd tried to kiss him.

"No," he said quickly. "I'm sorry."

She turned to unlock her door. "Thanks for dinner." She opened her door, intent on going inside and having a good pout.

He grabbed her arm. "Wait."

She pulled the door shut so her heat couldn't escape and looked at him. It was too cold to wait, but she couldn't exactly invite him inside.

"It's not that I don't want to kiss you." His words tumbled out one after another. "I do want to kiss you. It's just that, Kyra, where are we going?"

Uh ... "I wasn't asking you to marry me. It was just a kiss."

"Just a kiss," he said bitterly. "Well, I don't do that. To me, kisses mean something."

"That's not what I meant," she said quickly. Her nose was getting cold.

He stared at her. What was he waiting for? "So?"

She stared back.

"Where are we going? I don't want to get any more ... attached than I already am if you're just going to leave town in the spring."

Whoa. Wasn't it the woman's job to freak out about commitment? "I'm sorry, Brad. I'm really not thinking very far ahead right now." She was getting really cold. "Can we talk about this tomorrow?"

"I'll make it quick. I want to have a real relationship with you. And yes, I'm thinking toward marriage. Not yet of course. But if that's not the ultimate goal, then I don't see any point in trying to have a relationship. So, are you interested in having a relationship with me?"

"Are you seriously asking me that right now? Brad, I've had a pretty big day. For crying out loud, I can't make a decision that big right now in the cold with you staring at me."

"Fine. Let me know." He turned, and as he did, she caught sight of something awful in his eyes.

Hurt.

She'd hurt him.

Despite the cold, she followed him down the steps. "Wait."

He turned back to her.

"Of course I want a relationship with you, Brad. The more time I spend with you, the more I want that. You're amazing, and I'm so, so grateful that you exist and that you put up with me and that you seem to even like me—"

He laughed. "It's a little more than like."

"Okay. But I feel like you're asking me, right now, to decide what I'm doing next year, and I don't think that's fair."

"Sorry. But I think it's a bad idea to keep falling for you if you're just going to break my heart in June."

"Brad. I don't know what June's going to bring. I don't even know what tomorrow is going to bring. Can't we just enjoy today?"

He nodded. "Sure. As friends. I'll be your friend today. But that's it. I need to protect my heart."

"That's ridiculous."

"What?" He was shocked that she'd said that.

So was she.

"Why does our relationship status hinge on my professional plans? You want me to say that I'll stay here in nowhereland coaching a Division III team that doesn't even like me."

His expression softened. He'd heard her.

"But what if a DII job opens up? You act like I would break up with you and run away, but I wouldn't. If the relationship was working, if I still feel about you like I feel about you now, I would ask you to come with me!"

He stepped closer. "You would?"

"Yes!" Why was he being such a dingbat? Of course she would!

He stared at her for a long time, and she shifted her weight from foot to foot trying to get some feeling back into her toes. If she'd known she was going to have a heart-to-heart outside, she would've worn boots.

"Oh," he finally said.

"Oh."

His face broke into a smile, and he stepped to her, wrapped his arms around her waist, picked her up, and spun her around.

She giggled and patted his shoulders. "Put me down." She wasn't a minikin. He shouldn't be spinning her around like one. Someone would get hurt.

He did put her down, and then he brought his lips to hers, and they were the warmest, sweetest thing she'd ever touched. She accepted his kiss and then started to kiss him back, and her whole body melted into his.

She'd kissed a few men in her life. A med student and two lawyers, to be exact. Turned out professional prestige had nothing to do with kissing prowess. This kiss was out of this world. His lips made her feel unique, cherished, wanted ... his lips felt like security, like a vacation, like an ocean breeze ...

Like unconditional love.

He pulled away and smiled at her. "We should have done that sooner."

"I tried." She pointed at her steps. "Remember?"

He laughed and gave her another quick peck. "I need to get going before you get frostbite."

Oh yeah. She was cold. She'd forgotten.

"But see you tomorrow?"

She nodded, biting her lip, which was still tingling.

"Okay." He stepped back. "So you're like my girlfriend now? I can brag to my students?"

She laughed. "Yeah. I'm your girlfriend now." She pointed a finger at him. "But that doesn't mean that Meghan will get any more playing time. I know that's why you've swept me off my feet."

He laughed all the way to his car. She didn't stand around waving as he drove away, though. She ran inside, kicked her shoes off, and put her feet up on the register. Then she sat there smiling for quite some time.

February 4

Dear Frank,

Kyra got her job back! I knew it! One of the girls came forward and told the truth, so that's good!

The bad news is that Bruno has a lump on his shoulder. I know you would tell me not to panic, but I'm panicking. We have an appointment on Monday. I was angry they couldn't get us in sooner, but I guess lots of people have beloved pets with scary health needs. Anyway, I've only asked a few friends to pray about it because I know some people will think it's silly to pray about a dog. Especially with all the human suffering going on.

But I'm sure praying, Frank.

I don't know if I can survive losing him. I need his love, his companionship, but more than that, losing him will feel like losing another part of you, and I just don't know how I can do that. I don't have a lot of you left.

Oh, Frank, I'm sorry to be whiny. But I really, really hate this. Why did God have to take you?

Cindy

Chapter 40

Of all the people Kyra might have guessed would pop into her office on Friday afternoon, Cindy Harrington would be the last.

"I was in the neighborhood, so thought I'd come see where all the action is!" She was beaming. How could anybody be that happy all the time? Maybe she was faking it.

But she wasn't. Somehow Kyra knew that.

"Sorry, there's not much to see right now." There was no action. There was only Kyra watching Millsap College game tapes.

Cindy stepped into the room, but she didn't make it far. She stepped closer to the wall for a better look at the framed photos. Rows and rows of players gone by. "Wow, Fort George has quite a history, don't they?"

"Their first women's team was formed in 1971."

"Wow, right here in my town, and I didn't know hardly anything about it until you." She turned and gave her a huge smile. "I'm so glad you came along, Kyra."

"Thank you." Cindy's affection was warming but also slightly unsettling. Kyra wasn't used to being so … liked.

Cindy eyed a chair. "May I sit?"

"Of course." What was she up to? Did she have a burning desire to watch game tapes with her?

Cindy sat. "So I haven't gotten a chance to congratulate you."

"Oh. Well, thank you."

"You're welcome. Is everything okay? Is it really over?"

"I think so. One of the girls is sticking by her story, but it's pretty obvious that she's not telling the truth."

Cindy shook her head and clicked her tongue. "That poor young woman."

Kyra didn't know what to say to that. Leave it to Cindy to have compassion for that side of the story.

"How much pain do you have to be in to do that to someone?"

Kyra wasn't sure it was about pain. She thought it was about being a spoiled brat and loving drama. If either of those two traits was painful, Kyra didn't know it.

"I'll keep praying for her. So, how are things going with you and Brad?"

Oh, so that's why she was there? Kyra managed not to roll her eyes. She'd heard that Cindy liked to take credit for new relationships. Maybe she and Brad were going to be another notch on her belt.

"Things are good, I think. I really like him a lot." Why had she added that last part? Maybe she'd just wanted to say it out loud. It *had* felt good to say the words. She hadn't really told anyone about Brad. She'd had no one to tell except her father and stepmother, and she didn't think her father would be very impressed with Brad's chosen profession, so she was putting off that meeting for as long as possible and hoping Brad got promoted in the meantime.

"Good. I'm so happy for you. He's a good man. I've been looking for a good woman for him for some time."

Weird.

"You know who else is a good man?"

What? Had she come here to talk her *out* of Brad? "Uh ... no?"

"Colt Faro. Do you know him?"

"I don't think so."

"Well, you will if you stick around Greater Life for a while, and I hope you do. His wife died a few years ago, and I've been looking for a woman who might appreciate him ... and now that I know there's a whole other world nestled here on the Hartport shores ..." She looked around the room as if she could see the whole campus. "So I thought I'd ask you if you knew any other lovely single women. Either from here or from your old church?"

"How old is he?" She was pretty sure the youngest woman at her old church was still retired, but if Colt were a widower, then maybe he was older. Cindy probably didn't limit her matchmaking to a certain age bracket. If she did, she might run out of victims. Hartport wasn't a huge town.

"Not sure. I would guess mid-thirties."

"Then, no, sorry. I don't think I know anyone."

She looked so disappointed that it made Kyra take the question more seriously. "I can certainly keep my eyes open, though."

She still looked sad.

"Sorry, I don't socialize much on campus. I rarely leave this building, and most of the other coaches are men."

Cindy sighed. "It's okay. I knew it was a long shot."

Someone pounded on her door, and Kyra jumped.

Anyone that aggressive with knocking wasn't someone she wanted in her office, but the door was unlocked, and there wasn't exactly anywhere to hide. She stared at the door, not sure what to do.

The knock came again.

Cindy stood. "I'll get it for you." She gave her a look that said, *Don't worry, I got you*, but she wasn't sure what Cindy could do to protect her.

"Thank you," Kyra whispered, and Cindy opened the door.

A well-dressed man filled the doorway. He looked familiar, but Kyra couldn't place him.

He looked Cindy up and down, frowning, and then looked past her to Kyra. "I need to talk to you."

His voice sounded like thunder. Kyra stood, tried to look tough, and put on her professional I'm-not-scared-of-you face. She'd had to wear it many times before. "How can I help you?"

"You don't know who I am, do you?"

Please, God. Help me place him. "Of course I do. You're Saylor's father." *Thank you, Cindy, for mostly blocking his path.*

He stepped around Cindy and then looked back at her. "Is she your secretary?"

"Consultant," Kyra said quickly. It wasn't a lie. She was sort of a dating consultant. And if not that, then a spiritual consultant.

Kyra gestured toward a chair. "Please, have a seat." She didn't want him to stay for long, but he'd be less threatening if he was seated.

He didn't sit. "You must know why I'm here."

Not exactly. "I don't like guessing games. Why don't you tell me?"

This angered him. "You made big promises, young lady—"

She bristled but kept her mouth shut.

"My daughter agreed to come here because you were going to make her a big star."

And she'd tried. She really had. "Your daughter came here because I was the only one recruiting her." That was a polite way of putting it. She'd known way back then that Saylor would be problematic, but she hadn't cared. She had wanted her for her jump shot, not her personality.

Saylor's high school coach had cautioned Kyra that Saylor was difficult, but Kyra had ignored the warning. In truth, she'd thought herself a superior coach, thought she could coach the difficult out of Saylor. Boy, had she been wrong.

"That's a bald-faced lie!" he yelled.

Cindy took a few steps backward, toward the corner.

Kyra was so grateful that she was there.

As their visitor continued to spout off, Kyra promised herself that from now on, she would consider character as much as skill when recruiting.

When he had finished yelling, she calmly asked, "What is it you would like me to do, sir?"

His eyes widened. "Are you serious? I want my daughter back on the team, obviously!"

She hesitated. Was she understanding this correctly? "Saylor hasn't been removed from the team."

He took a step back. "That's not what Saylor told me."

"Well, then, I'm sorry to be the one to tell you that you've been lied to."

He narrowed his eyes. "She told me everything. I know about your little scandal, and I know that somehow, inexplicably, you're going to get away with it. Pretty obnoxious if you ask me. A man would never get away with that. And I know that Saylor had the courage to be the whistle blower—"

Kyra couldn't help it. She laughed aloud, which enraged him. "Sorry." She put her hand over her mouth.

"You think this is funny?"

She lowered her hand. "I do not." This whole thing had been the opposite of funny. "Here's what really happened, and there are plenty of witnesses if you'd like corroboration. Saylor got mad at me for kicking her ... *friend* off the team for drug use. So she made up a lie to get me fired. The truth came out as it always does"—she thought of Darren's sermon—"and her plan failed. But no one kicked her off the team. She is still on the roster. You'd have to ask her why she didn't show up for practice yesterday."

He was gobsmacked. Good. "Don't move." He whipped out his phone.

"I don't take orders from you." She picked up the phone to call campus security, just in case, but the door opened just then, and Dave stepped into the room. "Everything okay here?"

Chapter 41

"This is Saylor's father," Kyra said. "I'm trying to catch him up on recent events."

Dave didn't look surprised, so someone had already told him that the man was on campus.

The visitor barked his next order into his phone, telling the person on the other end to get to Kyra's office, and peppering his directive with vulgarity.

Kyra had a pang of sympathy for Saylor. But only a pang.

"Why don't you come into my office while we wait." Dave swung an arm toward the door. His tone suggested that it was more an order than an invitation.

"Is she coming?" He hissed at the word *she*.

"If she would like to."

Kyra did want to. She wanted to see Saylor's face when the train crashed.

Her father left the room, and Kyra followed, stopping in front of Cindy. "I'm sure you have things to do, but I'd appreciate it if you'd stick around for this."

She caught Dave's eye, and he looked befuddled. He had no idea who Cindy was and probably didn't want her privy to complicated athletic department dynamics.

"She's a friend," Kyra whispered. It might not make sense to him, but keeping Cindy around gave Kyra confidence, made her feel grounded in the truth of who she was.

Cindy followed her into Dave's larger office and sat beside her on the couch. Kyra couldn't wait to tell Brad about this. What, didn't everyone invite some random woman from church to all their work meetings?

Dave insisted that their visitor sit, and he finally complied. Then they all sat there awkwardly waiting for Saylor.

What if she didn't come? How were they going to get rid of this guy?

*If I were her, I'd steal a car and get as far away from this embarrassment as fast as I could. S*he wasn't Saylor, though. Not even close.

"Saylor!" Dave said loudly when she walked by his open office door. "We're in here."

Saylor backed up and looked into the room bewildered, her scan finishing with a confused stare in Cindy's direction.

"Come on in and have a seat," Dave said cordially.

Saylor slowly sank into the chair as if she feared it was going to bite her.

"What are you doing here?" she asked her father.

"What am I doing here?" he bellowed. "My daughter tells me she's been kicked off the team for being a whistle blower, I hop on the first plane I can catch!" He actually considered himself a hero. What a crock.

And Kyra was growing really tired of his use of the phrase whistle blower. If something bad had been going on, Saylor would have been the last person to blow the whistle.

For the first time in a month, Saylor didn't have a smug look smeared across her face. Instead, she looked scared. This made her look younger. Kyra wasn't enjoying this as much as she thought she would.

"Your coach here says that you haven't been kicked off the team. Is that true?"

She didn't answer him.

"Young lady! You need to start explaining yourself."

She seemed to shrink right there before Kyra's eyes.

"Dad, can we talk somewhere else?" Her voice trembled.

He nodded and started to get up.

"Wait," Kyra surprised herself by saying. "You two can talk all you want, but while you have us here, let's get this out in the open. Saylor, if you want to be on the team, you need to be at practice today. If you want to—"

"But I'm benched, right? You rebuilt the whole offense without me?" She looked at her father. "That's the same thing as kicking me off the team."

He frowned. "When did she do that?"

"Yesterday—" It was obvious that she was going for indignant, but he didn't let her.

"Yesterday? You mean when you didn't show up for practice? Saylor, did you blow the whistle on her or did you make up a lie about her?"

Her eyes flitted between her father and Kyra and then landed on the floor. It was answer enough.

Her father swore. Then he glared at her. "You will be at practice tonight, and you will do whatever she says to do for the rest of the season. And if that's ride the bench, then you will ride the bench. I am so—"

"I will not ride the bench!" she screeched. "Do you realize how embarrassing that is? To ride the bench of a Division III school?"

"I've heard enough," Dave said loudly and firmly. "Saylor, your coach has been more gracious than any other coach would ever be. You know she could sue you, right? She could press charges for slander!"

"And libel," Kyra added.

Saylor narrowed her eyes sassily.

"That social media posts of yours. I've got a screenshot."

The sassy look slid off her face.

"Saylor," Dave said, "Coach Carter was the only college coach to show interest in you. She made you a starter. She gave you a chance to really shine. And you blew it. Now she's not seeking any retribution *and* she's letting you stay on the team, and how do you respond? With blatant disrespect and more dishonesty. So I'm making an executive decision. Your words and actions are an embarrassment to Fort George, and as of right now, you are suspended from all athletic programs here. Indefinitely."

Kyra expected the father to protest, but he didn't. He stood up and glared down at his daughter. "Are you going to drop out now too, put the icing on the cake?"

She didn't say no.

Kyra didn't care what happened next to Saylor. She knew that Jesus still loved her, but she was content to let Jesus find someone else to minister to her. Kyra just wanted to get to practice and then get to Brad so she could tell him all about this—and then maybe kiss him some more.

Chapter 42

"You've got to be kidding me," Brad said, his eyes like saucers. "And Cindy was there for the whole thing?" He laughed and slapped his knee. "That's the best part!"

"I thought you'd appreciate that." Kyra was loving his response to her story.

"Wow, you have got one heck of a boss there, Kyra." He reached across the table and took her hand into his. "Maybe you shouldn't move on to a bigger and better school. You're not going to find a better boss."

He had a point.

Brad sighed and took a swig of his water. "Well, good riddance. At least now you can finish your season without constantly looking over your shoulder."

"Maybe." She still didn't fully trust Charlotte. Saylor might have cooked up the scheme, but it was Charlotte who had told the original lie. Charlotte had put the plan in motion. Saylor couldn't have done any damage without someone willing to tell that lie.

But Brad was partially right. It would be good to be rid of Saylor.

"So, Millsap College. Are they good?"

She nodded.

"Can you beat them without Saylor?"

"I think so. They'll beat us on the boards, so we just need to hit our shots the first time."

"You make it sound so easy."

She shrugged. "It can be." The truth was, she was unusually unstressed about Millsap. About the season, really. If they didn't beat Millsap, they would be out of the playoffs. A month ago, that would have devastated her. Now? Now things were different. Of course she still wanted to beat them. She still wanted to win the conference championship. But it no longer felt like life or death.

Her need to win had morphed into a want to win, which meant it no longer felt like a giant weight around her neck.

"Why was Cindy there in the first place?"

"She wanted to snoop about us," she said coyly.

"Oh yeah? What did you tell her?"

"That I'm crazy about you." It hadn't been those words exactly, but the meaning was the same. "She's telling people that she got us together."

He laughed. "Well, she did invite us to lunch. And more significantly, she has been praying for at least a year that I would find love."

"Really?"

"Yep. So I guess we can give her some credit."

Fine, we'll invite her to the wedding, she thought but didn't say aloud. "Why was she so worried about your love life?"

"Oh I'm just one person on her long list of lonely souls. She's praying for a bunch of us."

"Oh yeah, she mentioned someone else ..." She searched for the name. "Colt something?"

"Oh yes, Colt Faro. Nice guy. Kind of a weirdo."

She laughed. "What do you mean?"

"I guess weirdo is too harsh, but he's a big outdoorsman. And anytime I've seen him indoors, he's seemed so uncomfortable. Like he'd rather be out in the woods, as far away from people as possible."

She chuckled. "After the month I've had, I can't blame him."

Brad shrugged. "I'm not blaming him either. But I would go nuts without people around."

She raised an eyebrow playfully. "Don't like your own company?"

She hadn't meant it as a serious question, but he seemed to be taking it that way. "I don't know. I don't think that's it. I think I just really like people. I like to be entertained. I like to laugh. I like to make others laugh. Being around people makes me feel good." He smiled at her. "Especially you."

"Awww!" She giggled. "Well, Cindy asked me if I knew any women on campus, but I don't. I definitely don't know of an outdoorsy woman on campus."

"What, there's no professor who hunts and fishes and camps year-round?"

She laughed.

"What about the softball coach? Isn't she a woman?"

She nodded. "She is. But she's married."

"Bummer."

She laughed again. "Let's leave the matchmaking to Cindy. I'm not sure I have a knack for it."

"Fair enough. Sorry that I won't be there for your first game back."

"I'll be okay. It would be silly for you to drive all the way to Boston."

"Don't know why I can't hitch a ride in the team van."

She stared at him. Was he serious?

"Kidding."

Oh. Okay. "I'm not sure you'd want to. The team van is the worst part of the trip."

"Why's that?"

"Because I have to drive, and the girls are loud and obnoxious." She picked up her drink. "Reason number seventy-five to coach at a bigger school. They don't make the head coach drive."

Chapter 43

Kyra glanced at Millsap's score clock for the thousandth time. If she wasn't careful, they were going to lose this game. Daphne was shooting about two percent from the floor, and as Kyra had predicted, Millsap's giant front court was scooping up every rebound.

She looked at her bench. "Ella." She patted the empty seat beside her.

Ella didn't try to hide her surprise. She jumped up, pulled her warmup off over her head, and plopped down beside Kyra.

"You know this offense?"

"Of course."

"You know what the shooting guard does, where she goes?"

"Yes."

"Why don't you watch the next trip down, watch what she does."

"I don't need to. I know the offense."

"Good. Then get in there, and please hit those shots."

Ella ran to kneel in front of the scorers' table.

Maybe a break would help Daphne reset. Ella wasn't a great shooter, but she was better than Daphne was being right now.

The buzzer sounded, and the ref beckoned Ella onto the floor.

"Sorry, Coach," Daphne said on her way by.

Ugh. She didn't want apologies; she wanted performance. She opened her mouth to say as much but then snapped it shut. What good would that do? Daphne was already feeling bad. Maybe this wasn't the time to stack correction on top of frustration.

Oh wow, I'm really changing.

But thirty seconds later, when Ella did hit a shot, and then her team failed to go into the corresponding press, Kyra lost it and started screaming.

Easy, a voice in her head said, and she stopped, suddenly feeling self-conscious. She glanced at her bench, expecting them to be staring at her.

But they weren't. They were used to it.

Her eyes scanned the gym. No one was acting like she'd done anything wrong. They were all used to screaming coaches. It was part of the game.

So why did she suddenly feel so self-conscious?

Vicki drew a foul and went to the line for a one and one. The first shot bonked off the front of the rim.

Before Kyra could stop it, a frustrated "Come on!" erupted out of her. She clamped her mouth shut, now frustrated with herself. She sat down and put a hand over her mouth. She wanted to be a better coach. She wanted to be a better Christ-follower. But how was she going to change? She was born the way she was.

Vicki drew another foul and went to the line again. She missed again. Inside, Kyra was screaming. This was ridiculous. It was way too late in the season, way too late in their careers, to be missing freebies. But on the outside, she sat still and quiet.

Her assistant coach came and sat beside her. "Are you all right?"

The question startled Kyra. "Yeah, why?"

Tamara looked amused. "You look like you are trying to hold your breath."

She sort of was. "It's hard to explain." Her eyes followed the ball up and down the court. She didn't mind talking to Tamara, but she didn't want to miss anything either.

"You don't have to. I get it."

She looked at her quickly. "You do?" Kyra barely understood it, and she was living it.

"I think so." Tamara leaned forward and rested her hands on her knees. Now she was closer to Kyra's ear. "A bunch of people don't like the way you coach, tried to get you fired, and now you're trying to change the way you coach."

Yeah, that was pretty much it, minus the Jesus stuff.

Ella hit another shot. Kyra glanced at the clock. Good. They were up by six. This might happen.

"But you don't need to change the way you coach."

She looked at her again. "I don't?"

"No!" She sounded so sure. "You're a good coach. In my humble opinion, you should keep doing what you're doing, but ..."

Kyra looked at her expectantly.

"But maybe balance it out with some encouragement."

"Encouragement."

"Yes. I'm not saying lie to them. But I think they'll better receive your correction if they know that you care."

Kyra looked away so Tamara wouldn't see the tears in her eyes. She wasn't responding emotionally to Tamara's advice. She was responding to the spiritual resonance of it.

She better received God's correction because she knew that he loved her.

She looked out at her players. They were more than players. They were human beings, and she was supposed to love them. How different might things be if they thought that she did?

She leaned back in her chair. Oh wow. That would be a game changer.

Ella hit another shot.

Right now, Kyra didn't have to work hard to love Ella.

Chapter 44

On Sunday afternoon, the Fort George women's basketball team was celebrating in the Millsap locker room. They'd just won their second game against Millsap. They were happy to be back on top, and they were happy to be heading home.

Charlotte wasn't happy. She was trying to hide her face from everyone, especially the coaches, but she was crying.

Kyra pretended she hadn't noticed. She finished her talk and turned to leave the locker room.

Something stopped her. She looked back at Charlotte.

Oh boy.

Instead of leaving, Kyra waited until Charlotte was dressed and then said, "Charlotte, can I talk to you for a minute outside?"

Charlotte looked up in horror, but she grabbed her bag and came to the door.

Kyra stepped out into the hallway. She looked around to make sure no one was in earshot and then waited for Charlotte to make eye contact. "What's wrong?"

Charlotte's eyes widened. "What? Nothing. Northing's wrong." She sounded scared.

This pricked Kyra's conscience. Her asking a player what was wrong was so unusual that it struck fear in her heart? That was not a good thing. "Something's obviously wrong, Charlotte. Please tell me. I want to help."

Charlotte grimaced. She didn't believe her.

"Did I do something to upset you?"

Her eyes grew wider. She still didn't answer.

"Do you want to go get in the van and head home?"

Her face relaxed as she nodded.

"Good. Then you'd better tell me what's wrong, or we're going to spend the rest of our lives in this hallway."

Oh, was that almost a smile?

"I'm just … a lot of the girls are mad at me. And they're showing it."

Kyra let out a long breath. That made sense. "I will talk to them about it."

"No, don't," she said quickly. "Please. I don't want them to think I'm a tattletale."

Kyra smiled, surprised at how much compassion she was feeling for this young woman. "I am speaking from experience here, so don't feel like I'm lecturing you. But actions have consequences. Always. And sometimes we just need to suffer through them to get to the other side. The season's almost over. We're going to get our winning record back, and soon people will forget all about this season's drama."

She looked skeptical. "You think so?"

"I know so. I've lived through a lot of seasonal drama." She laughed.

Charlotte nodded. "Okay."

"Okay? Let's go get in the van." Kyra started to walk away.

"Coach?"

She turned back.

"Why don't you hate me?"

Oh boy. If she told the truth, she could get fired. A little voice in her head piped up, *So what?* and she almost laughed. Getting fired for Jesus would be pretty cool. She took a big breath. "I have messed up a lot in life, and God has always forgiven me. What kind of hypocrite would I be if I didn't forgive others?"

Charlotte stared at her for a long time. "I have a hard time believing you've ever messed up at anything."

"Believe it. It's true. No one is perfect."

"If you say so."

Kyra chuckled. "Come on. Let's get to the van and get home."

Charlotte fell into step beside her. "That church that invited us all to go? Gave out pretty cool presents." Her tone suggested this was a question. If so, Kyra didn't know the answer.

"Yeah?"

"Did you do that?"

"No, I did not. But it is my church." She hadn't realized that she'd decided Greater Life was her church, but now that she said the words, of course it was. It was more her church already that her previous church had ever been.

"Cool." And that was all Charlotte said to Kyra for the rest of the day. But it was enough.

As Kyra struggled with traffic to get the big, gompy van back out of Boston and onto the interstate, she thought about what she'd said about forgiveness. She needed to forgive Saylor too. And just like that, the weight lifted off her chest.

She felt freer than she'd ever felt.

And she couldn't wait to get home and tell the high school computer teacher all about it.

Chapter 45

Since Kyra's return to coaching, the women's team hadn't lost a game. They'd gone into the tournament with a decent seed and had easily worked their way to the championship game.

The conference tournament was being hosted by Reid State College, which was in Massachusetts, so Brad had stayed away from the fireworks.

But he didn't want to stay away from the championship, so he'd made the drive down. Alone. He'd invited some friends to come along, but he was the only one who seemed to think it was a good idea.

He got to the Reid State campus early, expecting it to be difficult to find a parking spot and a seat.

He had no trouble finding either.

Reid State hadn't lasted long in the tournament, and the home fans weren't interested in watching two Maine teams battle it out.

Fort George was up against Ashland, and very few people cared enough to go to the game. The gym was nearly deserted. To Brad, used to the packed home gym, it felt disorienting. With so many choices, he wasn't sure where to sit. He picked the top row directly across from the love of his life. He could lean against the wall and gaze down at her in all her glory.

He was so, so proud of her.

She had changed so much, and if he'd liked her before, now he was completely smitten. She still looked the same: her dark hair was pulled back into a too-tight professional bun; her makeup was movie star level; and the straight creases in her blue pantsuit were downright annoying. But her jaw wasn't tight, and her fists weren't clenched.

Kyra wasn't the only one who had changed. Her girls looked different too. They seemed lighter. A few of them were even smiling. Ella was singing along with the warmup music. The Kyra he'd first met would have nipped that in the bud, but the new Kyra was letting it slide. *Wonders never cease.*

The warmup clock went below two minutes, and Kyra beckoned them all to the bench. Even that was done with less panic than in the old days. He chuckled at the thought. The old days had only been two months ago.

But a lot had changed since then.

For one thing, he'd fallen in love. Of course, he hadn't told *her* that. Didn't want to freak her out, and he'd always believed that people couldn't fall in love that fast—until he'd lived it. Still, he was content to take things slow and enjoy them.

He stood for the national anthem and scanned the gym for a flag. He found it, a teeny, little thing nestled up in the corner of the gym, and put his hand over his heart.

One of the Ashland girls stepped up to the scorer's table and picked up a microphone. This was different. She started singing without any accompaniment, and he braced himself. It was always harder to sing a capella than people thought.

Sure enough, she didn't sound very good.

Being a high school teacher, he instantly worried about who might be mocking her, and he swept his eyes toward Kyra's bench.

But none of them were giggling or making faces. They were all staring respectfully at the flag.

Huh. What an honorable bunch of athletes. What integrity.

The national anthem picked up speed as she sang and soon finished to an applause surprisingly generous for the small crowd.

Brad sat for the fireworks.

And fireworks it was.

Daphne had the best game of her life, scoring twenty-six points, and local girl Ella, who'd been promoted to sixth man, added ten more. Brad only counted two turnovers during the whole game, and Kyra only screamed about one of them—and that one might have deserved it. Ella should have known by this stage in her career that she wasn't allowed to kick the basketball.

When the final buzzer sounded, Fort George had a fourteen-point lead.

The girls went nuts, jumping on top of each other and screaming.

Kyra looked like a true professional, striding across the gym and offering the opposing coach a handshake. Then she turned and headed back to her bench. She avoided the celebration.

Brad couldn't stand it anymore. Someone needed to mess up those creases. He climbed out of the bleachers, walked around the end of the court, giving her plenty of time to tell him not to, but she watched him coming and didn't protest.

He reached her, wrapped his arms around her, and spun her in the air. She giggled and patted his shoulders. "Put me down! You'll drop me!"

She was a tall woman, and it did take some effort to spin her, but he was still insulted. "Don't dis my manhood there, sweetie."

She giggled. "Just put me down, you big tough computer teacher."

When he did set her down, she held onto his arm with both hands. "Oh no! Now I'm dizzy."

"Wooo-hoo!" Ella called from the center of the court. "Way to go, Coach!"

Kyra's eyes grew wide. "Did you hear that?" she whispered.

"I sure did. Sounds like your team likes you, Coach."

"I wouldn't go that far."

"I would." He leaned in and kissed her, and Ella cheered some more, and this time, her teammates joined in.

Chapter 46

Kyra sat alone in her office staring at their championship trophy. It had been months, but she still hadn't gotten over the fact that they'd been knocked out in the second round of nationals. She'd really thought they would make it further than that—maybe even all the way. And maybe they would have if they'd still had Saylor's talent.

She was incredibly disappointed, but she was working on being less so.

Her phone rang, and she answered it quickly, grateful for the distraction.

"Hi, Ms. Carter. My name is Phil Blackwell. I'm the athletic director at White Spruce State University."

Her breath caught, and she sat up straight. "Hello! Please, call me Kyra."

"Hi, Kyra. Have you heard of White Spruce?"

"Of course." Who hadn't?

"Good, good. Do you know where we're located?"

Of course she knew that too. "I do."

He chuckled. "Good, well the fact that you're still talking to me suggests you haven't been scared off yet."

"Of course not. I'm in rural Maine. Can't be too much worse than that." She winced, hoping she hadn't offended him. Mainers were ridiculous about the pride they took in how tough their winters were. Maybe people from his neck of the woods were like that too.

He didn't sound offended. "I've never been to Maine. I haven't spent much time outside."

She might not either if she lived in his state.

"By that I mean outside of the state."

Oh!

"It's too much work to travel." He laughed. "Anyway, I'm sure Maine winters can be brutal. Our university is on the coast, so it doesn't get too cold. Anyway, I'd like to talk to you about a position we have open, but often our location scares off candidates, so I like to make sure we get the geography specifics right out there in the open."

She wasn't breathing. A position?

"The thing is, we've had a job opening posted for about six weeks now, and we haven't found a candidate yet that we're really excited about. So I was talking to Ravi Rogers"—it took her a second to place the name, but then she remembered that she'd worked with him at a previous college—"and he spoke very highly of you." He paused.

She couldn't think of a single word to say.

"So I started doing some digging, and it seems like you had a pretty rough season down there in Maine."

"We did."

"So I thought maybe you'd consider a move."

"Maybe ... What's the position?"

He laughed jovially. "I guess I should mention that, shouldn't I? We are looking for a head coach for the women's basketball team. The previous coach took his assistant coaches with him, so you'd be helping to hire the new ones."

She wasn't sure what to say. Was he asking her to apply or offering her the job? "That sounds intriguing."

He laughed. "Good to hear. So you'd consider it?"

"I would." A Division I school? She didn't care if it was on the moon!

"That's terrific!" He genuinely sounded excited. "Would you send me a resume, and if you're available next week, we'll fly you in for a formal interview and a tour."

"Sure!"

"Great. You can find my email address on our website. It was great talking with you, Kyra. I think this might be a good fit. I'll be in touch."

She thanked him, said goodbye, and then hung up the phone and stared at that trophy, her head spinning.

A Division I job? This was it. She forced herself to take a breath. This was what she'd been working toward. And it wasn't even a building program. White Spruce was solid. They hadn't won a national championship or anything, but they had made the tournament. She'd never thought about it before, but now she wondered how a school that far off the beaten path could convince a bunch of talented young adults to spend their college careers there. They must make pretty sweet offers.

She had a theory, and she searched the Internet for info about other programs at that college. Her suspicions were met. They didn't do very well in any other sport, but both men's and women's basketball were taken care of. She could assume then that the majority of the college's scholarships went to basketball. The idea of being able to offer a hard-working athlete a full ride gave her goosebumps. The idea of doing that again and again and again?

She wanted this job.

She stood up and grabbed her coat. She had to go talk to Brad. He might not be as excited about this as she was.

Chapter 47

"Y̶ou want to move to Alaska?" Brad nearly shrieked.

"I looked up the weather. It's warmer than it is here."

"But it's *Alaska!*" His eyes were huge.

Her excitement was leaking out of her like air from a tire. "If you don't want to, then it won't kill me to wait for the next opportunity." It hurt her to say the words. But even for the best job in the world, she didn't want to leave Brad behind. She wanted to marry him.

He studied her and then stepped closer and cupped her cheek in his hand. "You really want this, don't you? Your eyes are sparkling."

"It's insane they're even considering me—"

"No, it's not. Your record speaks for it—"

"Brad, listen to me. It is insane. I'm young for a DI job, and—"

"Maybe no one else is crazy enough to move to Alaska."

She playfully thumped him on the chest. "Will you stop? I'm not asking you to move to Siberia!"

He gave her a flirty smile, and his eyes got all smoldering. "Is that what's happening here? Are you asking me to follow you to Alaska?"

She shook her head. "Not yet. I'm asking if you would consider it. Because if you won't, then there's really no point in me pursuing it."

His expression grew tender. "I love you."

She smiled and leaned into him, planting her lips on his. When she pulled away, she said, "I love you too."

"You don't know how much it means that you're letting me be part of this decision."

"Of course."

"And though I really don't want to leave my students, and though I really don't want to leave my job, I would never stand in the way of your career. You have a gift. You are an amazing coach, and I would follow you anywhere. Well, maybe not to Siberia. Can we say anywhere in the US of A?" He grinned.

She was glad he hadn't specified the continental US. "Sure. We can say that. My second choice is a job in Wyoming."

He laughed. "Are there even any colleges in Wyoming?"

She put her arms around his waist and squeezed. "Yes, and I was only partially kidding. I would definitely take a job there. I'd love to see you in a cowboy hat."

He laughed harder. "No, no. I would follow you to Wyoming, but I am confident that I would look absolutely ridiculous in a cowboy hat." He kissed her again and then let go of her.

"Thank you. I know this is a huge sacrifice."

He shook his head. "Not huge. Like I said, you've got a gift. I mean, so do I, but I can use my gift anywhere. I'm sure there's a high school or a youth group where I can find new kids to help."

She hoped so.

"Dave must be devastated."

Uh ...

"What? You haven't told him yet?"

"I had to tell you first. If you said no way, then there was no use in getting Dave all wound up."

"Well, I'm honored to be the first to hear, but now you have to tell your number two."

She sat on the couch. "I don't think I need to tell him until after the interview. They haven't officially offered me a job yet."

"No, Kyra. You have to tell him."

She laughed. "That's not how this works. I don't need to tell him anything."

"Isn't he going to wonder where you are when you don't come into work for days?"

She shook her head. "It's summer vacation!"

"Ugh! Don't tease me."

She laughed. "You only have a week left."

"I know. I'm just playing. But seriously. It's summer, but coaches still work. Don't try to convince me otherwise."

"You're right. We do. But loads of us take days off, and he doesn't pay any attention."

He was staring at her.

"Why is this so important to you?" She didn't understand why he was so vested in Dave's interests.

He shrugged. "I like Dave. He's been good to you. I think you should be up front with him the whole way." He held his hands up. "But it's your career. I'm not going to try to make you do anything."

He was right. It was her career. But she also respected his opinion. "Fine. I'll tell him."

Brad looked at his phone. "Do you think he's in his office?"

"No idea."

Brad grabbed his keys. "Let's go find out. Then we'll get some enchiladas."

She grudgingly followed him to his car. She didn't think it was a bad idea, necessarily, and she wasn't scared to face Dave. He'd known when he hired her that she was on her way up. She just really didn't want to upset him for nothing.

Of course, if she was honest with herself, this probably wasn't going to be nothing. Phil Blackwell had sure sounded serious. If she didn't totally botch the interview, she was pretty confident she'd be offered the job.

Dave wasn't in his office, but she found him in the uniform locker.

"Inventorying?"

He was surprised to see her. "We're missing some uniforms. Was hoping they'd only been misplaced. What can I do for you?"

She thought he should sit down, but telling him to was a bit arrogant.

"Go on, spit it out. You know I'm ready for it, right?"

"What, did they call you?"

"Nope. I don't even know who *they* is. But I have known people would try to filch you. I'm surprised it's taken this long."

"*They* is White Spruce State."

His head snapped up. "Holy smokes!"

"Yeah."

"Head coach?"

She nodded.

His eyes were giant. "Kyra, congratulations."

"Well, I don't have it yet. They want to interview me next week."

His eyes stayed wide, but his expression grew sadder, and he looked away. "I've known since I met you that we would lose you, but that doesn't mean I want to."

"I know. I'm sorry."

"Oh no, no need to be sorry." He pushed some boxes around and made room for a seat on the bench, which he took. He looked up at her. "This is how it works. We're a small school. We can't expect to get the best. We're lucky to have had you this long. But selfishly, I sure have enjoyed winning these championships. I like having something to be proud of."

He couldn't have been too proud this winter, but she was glad he'd had some good moments at least.

He smiled. "I don't want to stand in the way of your dreams, but if you do get an offer, would you speak to me before you say yes?"

She stared at him, not quite following. "What if they offer while I'm standing in their gym?"

He looked down at his hands. "Good point. I guess that was too big of an ask. Okay, let's do it this way ... Kyra, if you stay on for one more season, I'd like to offer you a fifty percent raise for that year."

What? That was insane.

"I know that it's still not as much as they're going to offer you, but I can't go any higher."

"Wow, Dave. I don't know what to say."

He waved her off. "Go. Enjoy your first-class flight. Take the job if that's what you think is best, if that's what you want. Don't feel an ounce of obligation to me or to this school. But if you *do* feel like sticking around, well, that raise is waiting for you."

Chapter 48

Kyra dragged herself out of bed. She'd hardly slept at all the night before. Her mind was spinning, and though she was excited about the possibilities of a big school with big money and world class athletes, she was also unreasonably sad about leaving Fort George.

She didn't want to leave her girls. Or Dave. Or Greater Life.

And while she thought that Brad would go with her, there was still this niggling doubt. Would he? Would he really? And if he did, would he resent her for it?

Part of her wanted to lie in bed and keep trying to sleep, but that wasn't in her nature. The sunlight was pouring in through her bedroom window, making it too bright to sleep. And if she pulled a blanket up over her eyes, she would die of heat stroke.

Sleep or no sleep, it was time to get up.

She wanted to be at the airport by two for her four o'clock flight. After a quick layover at JFK, she had a six-hour flight to Seattle. She could sleep then.

She padded her way to the coffee pot. She usually enjoyed flying, so why wasn't she more excited?

Her coffee poured into her favorite mug, she settled into the corner of her couch with her Bible and her book of devotions. She'd ordered a copy of the book that Cindy was giving out to basketball players. And though Kyra's playing days were well behind her, she was still getting a lot out of the book of devotions.

Her phone beeped, and though it was tempting to put the Bible down and pick up the phone, she managed not to. She wasn't always successful, but she tried not to interrupt a conversation with God to talk to someone else.

But then her phone beeped again.

And again.

And again.

Then it rang.

"Oh for crying out loud!" She grabbed the phone. "Sorry, God."

It was Cindy.

Frowning, she checked her texts. Yep, those had all been from Cindy too.

"Hello?"

"Good morning! Sorry for the short notice, but you need to go to the awards ceremony this morning."

"What awards ceremony?"

"At the school!"

As much as she loved Cindy, she was getting frustrated. "What school?"

"Freedom Academy. They have an awards ceremony. And it starts at ten. And I think you should be there."

She looked at the time. It was almost a two-hour drive to South Portland, which meant she had to leave for the airport by noon. "How long is the assembly?"

"I don't know." Now she was the one sounding impatient. "I'll be there in five."

"Be where?"

"At your house."

"What? Cindy, I'm still in my pajamas!"

"Well you've got five minutes to get out of them." She hung up.

Kyra stared at the phone in disbelief. Cindy was nuts! No woman could get ready to go out in public in five minutes. So she didn't try. She finished reading the Scripture that went with the devotions, and then she prayed. "God, I am a nervous wreck. Thank you for this opportunity. It's the best one I could have hoped for, and way ahead of schedule. And I am excited. But I'm sorry if I'm not grateful enough. My emotions are all mixed up. This is what I'm supposed to do, right? Please help me take my emotions out of my decision making and do what is best ... actually, help me do what you want me to do. However this turns out, I want to do what you want. I want peace—"

There was a knock at her front door. "Thank you, Father. In Jesus' name I pray. Amen." She got up and went to the door.

Cindy stood there in the sunshine. "You're still in your pajamas!" She was incredulous, and there was laughter in her voice. She gently pushed her way inside. "Hurry! Get dressed."

Kyra glanced at the clock on her wall. "I can't possibly get to the school by ten. Why do you want me to go to this thing, anyway?" She only knew one person at that school. Two if she counted the superintendent who happened to be her pastor.

"I'll tell you on the way."

Kyra stared at her. She wasn't doing this. "Cindy, I love you, but I'm saying no."

The joy fell out of Cindy's expression, and she stepped closer. "Please trust me. You need to go."

"What? Why would I possibly *need* to go to a tiny Christian school's awards ceremony?" And then she knew. It had something to do with Brad. "What is it? Is Brad getting an award?"

Cindy only stared at her.

"Fine. But we're going to be late." She showered as fast as she could and got dressed quickly, but then her progress slowed down with the makeup.

Cindy pounded on her bathroom door, and Kyra yanked it open. "What?"

"You look great. Come on."

"Cindy, I only have makeup on half of my face."

Cindy started grabbing her makeup off the counter. "Come on. You can do the other half on the way."

Horrified, Kyra put her hands over Cindy's. "I've got it." She took the makeup out of Cindy's hands, but then put it in a pile. "If you'll give me a second, I need to brush my teeth. Or would you like me to do that during the assembly?"

Cindy backed away. "No, no. Go ahead."

Kyra rolled her eyes. Then she brushed her teeth in record time, put her hair up into the worst bun of her life, and grabbed her makeup. When she spun around, she almost ran into Cindy. "You're going to owe me for this—whatever this is."

"You'll thank me later. Come on." Cindy grabbed Kyra's purse off the hook by the door. Kyra's hands were full. When she tried to shut the door behind her with her foot, Cindy did it for her.

They got to the school at two minutes past ten, and Kyra was still applying mascara.

"Come on, you look great!" Cindy started to get out of the car.

Kyra ignored her and kept working on her eyelashes.

Cindy came around to her door and ripped it open. "Come on!" She yanked on Kyra's arm, causing Kyra to paint a large streak of mascara across her temple. "Oops." She didn't feel bad for long. "Come on. Put your hair down. It will cover it."

She couldn't put her hair down. It was all poofy. It would look like nineties Reba hair. She licked her finger and tried to get the mascara off her skin, but it was waterproof. Fine. She took her hair down and swept some of it over her temple. Oh no. She looked terrible.

Chapter 49

T he assembly had started when Kyra and Cindy got into the gym. They stood against the back wall and watched an endless stream of trophies being handed out.

Kyra grew tired. If this were this many trophies, they didn't mean much.

She could have done her makeup ten times by now. She looked at her phone. She needed to get back to her place and get pointed toward the airport. She was leaning over to whisper this to Cindy when Cindy elbowed her in the ribs.

"Ow!"

"Shh. Here it comes."

A man in a nice suit went to the podium, replacing the man Kyra assumed to be Freedom Academy's principal.

The man put some papers down and then leaned on the podium, eying the crowd. "Good morning. My name is John Jenson, and I am here representing Christian Teachers of America. We are an organization made up of Christian teachers and administrators, and we exist to support, edify, and equip outstanding teachers across the country." He glanced down at his papers.

"Thanks to generous members and supporters, each year we award a grant to an outstanding teacher. Past recipients have included kindergarten teachers as well as advanced placement teachers."

Kyra realized what was going on. Oh, how awesome. Her heart swelled with pride.

"Steve Burbank, a band teacher from Logan, Colorado, used his grant to buy new instruments for any student who wanted one and to hire outside musicians to come give special lessons to the students. Wyatt Bellamy of Sandy, Ohio, used his grant to take his math team to an NFL game. He had been teaching them how to use statistics to predict outcomes in sports. His students got to meet Tim Tebow! And last year, Tammy Garrity, a third-grade teacher in California, used her grant to add a library to her elementary school. These are just some examples of how a grant from CTOA can be used, but it is up to the recipients how they wish to use them. We only stipulate that they be used to benefit the students at the winner's school. Now, you may be wondering how we select our grant winners. In fact, you're all probably wanting to apply." He laughed at his own joke.

"But we don't take applications. Instead, we ask administrators and pastors for nominations, and we get hundreds of them. It's hard to choose, believe me. There are a lot of teachers doing a lot of great work in this country. But of all the good options, we pick one each year. Now, this person has to be a good teacher. We ask their bosses to confirm that they are doing their job and getting results. But that's only the beginning. CTOA strives to recognize teachers who go beyond their subject matter, teachers who go beyond teaching. We look for teachers who *disciple* their students, teachers who live out their faith in a way that the students notice. So, let's review."

He held up one finger. "First, we solicit nominations. We got this one from your pastor, who is also your administrator. These grants don't always go out to Christian schools, by the way." He looked down at Darren. "Thank you, Pastor, for your nomination."

John Jenson held up two fingers. "Second, we ask administrators a series of questions. And third"—three fingers now—"we check with the students. Here are some things that your students said about this year's CTOA grant recipient." He looked down at his paper and read, "'This teacher has changed my life. I've always been a Christian, but he made me understand how to make following Jesus a real thing, an important thing, not just a thing we talk about.'" He paused before the next one. "'This teacher is my favorite teacher. He is so fun and funny, and he showed me that being a Christian doesn't have to be all serious all the time. I always thought Christianity was boring, but not in his classroom.'" He looked up to see if his words were having an effect.

They certainly were on Kyra. It was a good thing that mascara was waterproof.

"And this Freedom Academy graduate says, 'I am in my third year of computer science at University of Maine at Orono.'" Some of the people in the audience knew then that Brad was the winner and began to cheer. John Jenson talked over them to finish the quotation, "'I don't think I would have gone to college if it weren't for this teacher. Not only did he help me decide to go, but he stayed after school for hours helping me fill out scholarship applications. Because of him, I only need to pay for my books.' And one more. This one might be my favorite. 'I came to Freedom because I'd been kicked out of public school. I hated everything about Freedom Academy. How strict it was. How small and weird it was. How terrible our sports teams are. But this teacher welcomed me and then he wore me down. And then one day, hours after school had ended, he helped me pray my first prayer to Jesus, and I've been following Jesus ever since. I don't want to think about what my life might be like if I'd never met this teacher.'" John Jenson looked up. "Ladies and gentlemen, this year's recipient of the CTOA grant is your Mr. Brad Foster."

The place erupted. All the students leapt to their feet, and the staff soon followed. There was shouting, whistling, clapping, and even stomping.

Kyra moved so she could watch Brad walk up onto the stage.

John Jensen gave him a quick hug and then handed him an envelope and a plaque, which Brad held up for all to see, which made the cheers intensify.

In fact, the cheers wouldn't stop.

After a few minutes of crazy chaos, the principal went back up on stage and started telling people to calm down and sit down.

The students resisted for quite a while, but then he told them they would be late to lunch if they didn't sit down and close their mouths.

They sat, a few stray whistles accompanying the rustle of a few hundred butts hitting chairs.

"Thank you, Freedom family," Brad said into the microphone. Then he laughed awkwardly. It was adorable. "I don't really know what else to say."

A tall kid near the back yelled, "Say you're going to take us to the Superbowl!" and everyone started cheering again. Again the principal started hollering, and soon the noise died down.

"I am so, so honored ..."

Kyra felt bad for him. As if he had a speech prepared for such a thing.

"I guess I'll just say that I would never want to do all this if it weren't for you guys. You kids really are the best, and that's why I do the job I do. So, thanks for being awesome." He held the plaque up again as he stepped back from the podium.

As the applause erupted again, Kyra caught Cindy staring at her.

"Thank you," Kyra mouthed.

Cindy looped her arm through Kyra's and gave it a squeeze, and Kyra was overwhelmed with love for this place that she'd hated for so long.

There was something special about Hartport. Of course it was Brad. But it was more than Brad.

Brad made this place special, but she also thought that this place made Brad special too.

And she was going to leave it?

June 7

Dear Frank,

I think she's going to stay. Phew! I promise I wasn't being selfish. I wasn't trying to keep Brad around for myself or for the kids. But she had to see who he really was before she made the decision, and now she's seen it. And I think I could see it in her eyes. I don't think she's going to want to move away now.

We'll see, of course.

Bruno continues to do well. No signs of any lumps coming back, thank God. I really need to keep him here with me for as long as possible, so if you can pull any strings up there, please do.

Your azaleas are finally blooming. They look beautiful. They are so beautiful, they're sad.

I love you, Frank. I'm trying to enjoy your favorite time of year, but it's not easy. I hope it's always spring in heaven.

Cindy

Chapter 50

When Brad stepped out of his classroom, he found Kyra waiting in the hallway. He almost yelped in surprise. "What are you doing here?"

"I thought maybe you'd like to go somewhere and celebrate."

"Kyra! Did you miss your flight?"

"Let's go somewhere, and I'll explain."

His heart leapt with hope. Had she changed her mind? *Don't get too excited*, he told himself.

He accepted her quick kiss and her hand and then followed her out to her car. The sunlight hit his face like a second kiss, and the birds were chirping. Every spring sort of caught him by surprise. It was as if, year after year, his soul said, *Phew. We made it out of winter. That was a close one.*

She drove toward House of Salsa. He tried to ask questions, but she kept shushing him.

She wouldn't tell him anything until they'd ordered their food. Then she took his hands in hers. "I called the college and told them that I was very, very honored, and that I would love to coach there one day, but that I wasn't ready to leave Fort George."

Relief washed through him with a force that surprised him. He didn't think he'd been that reluctant to go, but maybe he had. "Really? Why?"

"Brad, seeing you with those kids ... I can't take you away from that."

No, no, no. "You have to call them back."

"What? Why?"

"I can't let you give this up for me. This is what you've been working for forever. This is who you are."

"I know, but ... I think I've changed."

"No. You need to call them back. I can work with kids anywhere. Kyra, your gift is *special*."

"*Your* gift is special!" she nearly screeched. "I know that now! I'm sorry I didn't know that before."

He stared at her. How was he going to get through to her? "I can't let you do this."

"You can't *let* me?"

Oh my salt, are we going to fight over this?

"Brad, what if I promised to go later?"

"What?"

"Someday. Someday I want to coach at a bigger college. But not today. I just ... I didn't have peace with it. I don't think it's what I'm supposed to do. I think I'm supposed to stay in Hartport, coach Ella and Meghan another year. Watch you be awesome at Freedom Academy for another year."

He hesitated, and the relief tried to creep back in. "So, it's not just about me?"

She shook her head. "It's not. I promise. I mean, it's mostly about you." She laughed. "But not entirely. I want to stay here another year. Maybe more. It feels like home right now."

"Okay. If you're sure."

"I'm so sure." And she looked it. "I just ... I'm starting to think that maybe life is too short to constantly be climbing the ladder. I mean, I'm not jumping off the ladder or burning it down. I'm just pausing on my current rung. I want to enjoy it here for a while. Besides, Dave is giving me a huge raise."

"He is? That's awesome! Congrats! Wish Darren would give me a huge raise."

She wiggled her eyebrows. "You're famous now. Maybe you've got some leverage. Anyway, let's enjoy our summer here! We live in Vacationland, for crying out loud, and have I ever taken a vacation? No! Never! I think it's time I did. We can vacation *together*. Beaches. Lobster. Sunshine. Kayaking ..." Her eyes shone as she made her list.

"That sounds heavenly."

"But first, I have a confession to make." Her smile faded.

Oh boy. "Okay."

"I looked down on you when we first met. I actually thought I was too good for you because of your job. I'm so sorry. I was such a fool. You aren't doing that job because you can't find a job that the world thinks is better. You're doing that job because you're doing God's work there. I'm so sorry I didn't see that."

He squeezed her hands. "You're one hundred percent forgiven." She didn't say anything else, so he said, "Kayaking? Really? I didn't know you kayak."

"I don't. But I've always thought it looked like fun. Especially in the ocean."

"Fun. And dangerous."

She laughed. "Really? Well, then we don't have to go kayaking."

"No, no, let's. I have a great idea." It was better than great. It was the best idea he'd ever had. "My cousin kayaked from Falmouth out to Clapboard Island. We could do that, have a little picnic there and then kayak back?"

She shook with excitement. "Yes! Let's do that as soon as you get out of school!"

His excitement matched hers. But that part wasn't his great idea. Right then he decided that on Clapboard Island, he was going to ask Kyra Carter to marry him. He'd been planning to do it during a basketball game. It only seemed fitting. But now he didn't want to wait till winter. "Yes. It's a date."

"I was so, so proud of you today, Brad. You are such a great man."

Now he felt a little uncomfortable. "Not really. But you make me greater. And you won't find a man who loves you more."

She stood and leaned across the table to kiss him. Her lips were warm and sweet, and she smelled like wild roses. She broke the kiss but hovered there, looking into his eyes. "And you won't find a woman who loves you more either. So we're a perfect fit." She sat down.

Yep. There was no such thing as a perfect person, for sure. But she was the perfect person for him.

Epilogue

Vic stumbled out of the woods into a clearing and startled when she saw flames.

A campfire, surrounded by people. Good. She needed extra eyes. She gave extra weight to her footsteps so they would hear her coming, but they were still shockingly unobservant. "Hi!" she called out.

"Why, Vic Collins!" Cindy Harrington jumped up from a folding chair and hurried to her.

Relief washed over Vic at the sight of Cindy's familiar, loving face. Plus, Cindy would understand what she was going through. But before Vic could tell Cindy what was wrong, Cindy was dragging her toward the fire.

"Everybody, you need to meet my good friend!" Cindy said with delight.

One of the men rolled his eyes. "Everyone is your good friend, Cindy." But then he smiled at Vic. "Hi, Vic. I'm Lincoln. Nice to meet you."

The little girl in the smaller chair beside him scrunched up her nose. "Vic? That's a weird name."

Lincoln gave Vic an apologetic look. "Honey, that was rude. It's probably short for Victoria." He looked behind Vic as if expecting someone else to come out of the woods. "Are you okay?"

Before Vic could answer his question, Cindy corrected him. "Not Victoria. It's short for Victory."

"Wow, that's the coolest name ever," a woman said.

Vic looked in the direction of the compliment and was momentarily distracted from her grief and terror. Despite multiple empty chairs, a couple sat on a log, their limbs so intertwined they were nearly tangled. They were obviously madly in love, but what Vic noticed was the posture and presence of the woman.

The woman was smiling at her. "I'm Kyra."

Kyra was tall, strong, and confident, and yet this man was obviously gaga for her. Huh. That wasn't how it had worked out in Vic's life. She'd figured out that men didn't like tall, strong, confident women. And yet there they were.

Their happiness gave her grief a jagged edge that cut into her without warning. She nearly gasped at the pain of it, and tears sprang to her eyes.

This made her angry. She hated crying. She especially hated crying in front of people.

"So what are you doing wandering around in the woods all alone?" Cindy finally asked. And then, before Vic could answer, "I mean, I know you love wandering around in the woods, but ..." Her tee-heeing quieted when she finally noticed the pain in Vic's eyes. "Sweetie, what's wrong?"

Vic faced the group and took a big breath. "I really need your help."

Books by Robin Merrill

GREATER LIFE ROMANCE
Forgive and Remember
A Good Day to Live
No Time to Win

NEW BEGINNINGS
Knocking
Kicking
Searching
Knitting
Working
Splitting

SHELTER TRILOGY
Shelter
Daniel
Revival

PIERCEHAVEN TRILOGY
Piercehaven

Windmills
Trespass

Made in the USA
Middletown, DE
21 July 2022

69817829R00132